# Conflict Lessens

## By Harlowe Frost

ISBN eBook: 978-1-959981-55-8
ISBN paperback: 978-1-959981-56-5

Editor: Weslee Imrisek
Developmental Editor: Angela Grimes
Cover Art: Getcovers.com
Formatting: Huckleberry Rahr

# Books In the Magic Of The Galaxy Series

### Series 1: Viera Kor

Book 1: Galaxy Lessons

Book 2: Magic Lessons

Book 3: Conflict Lessens

## Acknowledgement

This book is the end of the trilogy. I am in talks with my writing team to create more in this world. You are welcome to find me on facebook or my website to let me know your opinion one way or the other.

As always, I am forever grateful for the help, encouragement, brilliance, and laughs I get from wise and wonderful people, such as Weslee Imrisek, Angela Grimes, Nicole Maness, Lawrence Henry, Gavin Rahr, and many others. Without these people, this series would not be what it is.

As much as I love writing, the people who this crazy world has brought into my life is even better! I love you all!

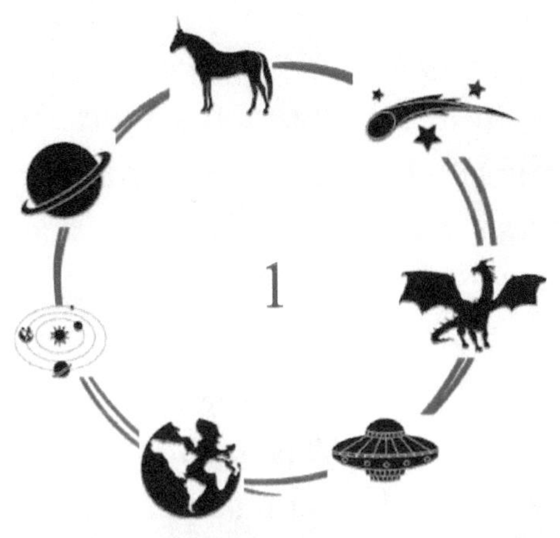

## Out of Sight, Out of Mind

### Viera

"So, you called us here for an emergency meeting for a single alien bug, Ms. Doeth?" The government man's lip twitched as he tapped his pen on the long mahogany table—too long for the few people attending the meeting. His short dark hair and brown eyes looked dull, as exciting as his personality. He held his face in a generic, if not very plastic looking, welcoming position. "You know we're busy. Just because you have access to government officials, and somehow got the position as alien liaison at your tender age, doesn't give you the right to rile up the troops at any drop of the hat."

Betsy's mouth tightened. Viera thought her friend might lay a curse on the man. *Can she lay curses? Is that even a thing?* Betsy straightened and narrowed her eyes. "Mr. Pilsner, I don't know what my age has to do with anything, but I think you should consult your predecessor's notes. As for *one alien bug* as you so nicely summarized, the krottel are a hive species. One bug means there are more we need to worry about. If not on-planet, then they'll be here soon. We know they want to invade our planet—"

"But they won't, right?" he interrupted. He leaned back, probably not wrinkling his expensive-looking black suit. "Your report—this report," he tapped a folder with the end of his pen, "the one you submitted after your friend here left the planet and got our planet on the radar of these creatures ... you know what report I'm talking about?"

Viera blanched. *Betsy submitted reports to this asshole? She gave him reports about me? Me and my situation? He knows I was taken aboard Thorn's ship over spring break and whisked away to Torville Station Number Six? Goodness. What else does this jerk know? How many people have heard or read about the chanzii, teleportation, and do they know what GPS really stands for?*

Betsy smirked. "Mr. Pilsner, you've been on this job for, what, two years?"

"Yes, what about that?" He narrowed his eyes at her, seemingly uncertain where she was going. Viera wasn't sure either, but Betsy's attitude had clearly shifted.

"You have other responsibilities. Working with me and the other Pillars is only a small piece of your duties. Am I correct?" She asked the question so lightly, as if she didn't have a care in the world. *It's a trap! Run, government man, run! Even my students would know to be scared.*

"Yes, Ms. Doeth, I have real responsibilities. You're barely a blip on my radar."

Betsy's smile grew. "Perfect." She pulled out her phone and started typing.

"What are you doing, Ms. Doeth?" He sounded bored, but maybe a bit curious. Nothing he said or did convinced Viera he cared one way or the other. *Betsy warned me not to probe inside these walls and read anyone, but can he really be this blasé? No one can be that simple.*

Betsy ignored him.

He leaned forward, face tightening, head tilting.

Viera glanced back and forth between them like a silent tennis match. *What is Betsy doing? We're here for a reason, right? Shouldn't we—she—be doing more?*

After a few minutes, Mr. Pilsner, who had finally stopped fidgeting, started tapping his pen on the table again. Betsy continued to ignore him. *Is she playing on her phone? Is she seeing how far she can push him? Is this a test?*

Finally, Mr. Pilsner sighed, long and loud. "Ms. Doeth, I'm really a very busy man. I have other appointments—important work to do. If you're going to play on your phone, then I'm afraid I have to leave."

There was a beat of silence, and then Betsy casually looked up from her phone, as if surprised the man was still in the room. "Mr. Pilsner, as my friend would say in her other job, you're dismissed. I have requested," she tilted her head in his direction, "a new point of contact from your boss. I made sure he understood that anyone assigned to this position has a basic working knowledge of respect. If I ever bring this person in front of the aliens and they act like you," she barked out a laugh, then shook her head, "you wouldn't survive the meeting."

"What?" He blustered. "You can't fire me. You don't have that kind of authority."

"Oh, but that's what you don't understand, Benedict. I do. I have the ultimate authority here. I am also older than anyone in this building. I outrank *everyone* here. You should've read the file." With a snort, Betsy went back to her phone.

Benedict snapped his eyes to Viera. *I wonder if his friends call him Benny. His name is so uptight. Then again, so is he.* "Are you older than dirt as well, Ms. Kor?"

It took a lot of effort not to roll her eyes at him. "I understand basic respect and proper questions, Mr. Pilsner. I'm not sure how you were assigned this position; it is one of honor and prestige. The fact that you would squander it baffles me. I would say it was nice meeting you, but we both know that's a lie. I do hope you mature and grow from this."

As she finished her words, the door opened, and an even younger man walked in. If Benedict was in his thirties, the other man was at most thirty. He had dark auburn hair that matched the freckles that ran across his cheeks and nose. His sparkling blue eyes took in the room before he walked up to Betsy. "Ms. Doeth, my name is Juk Hopkins. You can call me Juk or Mr. Hopkins, whichever you prefer. I know you've called my last three predecessors, barring Benedict, by their first names, so I'd be happy if you called me Juk. I've read all your files and am thrilled to be called in to meet you."

Betsy twined her fingers together in front of her face and gazed at the man. "Why did you read the files if I was working with this lout?"

"I was assigned as back-up for the times he wasn't available. We were both given the files and told to learn what we could." He stood so tense, Viera's muscles ached in sympathy.

"Three predecessors?" Benedict bellowed. "For fuck's sake, Juk, what are you talking about? These women are as young as us. Are you daft?"

Juk slowly turned to his colleague. "Right. You're needed upstairs."

"Are you going to answer my question?"

He shook his head. "As in, they requested your presence *now*. If you want to keep your job, you should run."

The color drained from Benedict's face as he quickly gathered his stuff and scurried from the room.

Betsy sipped the glass of water they'd each been offered when they'd arrived. "Okay, Juk, sit. And relax before you have an aneurysm, or some other medical mishap."

Juk chuckled and sat, placing a file, a pad of paper, and a few pens and pencils on the table. "Okay, what were you discussing?"

Betsy sighed and looked at Viera.

Viera shrugged. "There is an alien species called the krottel. They're a bug-like creature that wants Earth for themselves. Though the Elders, a group of aliens with clout, told them to back down, we found a krottel on an island off the Gulf Coast."

Juk put down his pen and rubbed the back of his neck. "Okay, so you found a single bug. But did you find more? A hive?"

Betsy's hands fisted but she spoke calmly. "No, but the bugs can speak telepathically. We're sure that bug was a scout and the rest plan to invade."

Juk went back to taking notes. "The rest? All of the krottel, or like, a single ship? What sort of scale are we talking about? And when?"

Betsy spoke slowly. "All of them. If not now, then soon. If you've read my recent reports, you know that they need a planet and think that Earth will be their salvation. They want to evacuate all of us and take over the planet. If we won't leave, they'll take more extreme measures. They aren't above extermination. They're ignoring the Elders and seeing this planet as their species' one hope of survival. To the krottel, it's them or us, life or death, and Earth is the prize."

Juk froze for a moment, then bobbed his head. "Did the bug tell you this? Do you have a way to communicate with a single entity?"

Viera's jaw tightened. Though Juk was more respectful, they weren't going to get any further with him than Benedict. They were just going to fail more pleasantly.

"I'm using the facts from what happened to Ms. Kor on Torville Station Number Six and what I know of the krottel. We need to be prepared."

He slowly put down the pen. "It's not that I don't believe you. I do, but for now, with just one bug found, and it now completely contained, I don't know that we have the resources to do more than what we've been doing: monitor the skies for enemy ships. With the chanzii ship orbiting and aware of what's going on as well, I feel we're well protected."

"More needs to happen," Betsy insisted. "It's going to be an invasion. More than that, the chanzii ship will be gone next week. The paperwork has already been submitted, so you should know what's going on."

"That's right—taking the octopus girl and her parents to the space station." Juk nodded. "Will the two of you be going, too?"

Viera smiled, excited for the upcoming trip. "I will. The last day of school is coming up, so I'll be free to travel." She shot her friend a quick look. "And traveling out of Wisconsin, my home state, is always exciting."

Betsy smiled. Until spring break, Betsy had always teased that she never traveled more than a dozen miles from home. Now she was in Washington, D.C. for this meeting, and next week she was off for a trip in space.

Many things had changed in only a few months.

"Well, great. Thank you for being so diligent in your work, Ms. Doeth, but I really feel for now this threat ... well, isn't. It was only one bug. We will make sure to double our space monitoring protocols, but beyond that, I'll be sleeping just fine tonight."

Betsy gave him a tight, almost patronizing smile. "Well, Juk, that makes one of us." She stood up, and Viera followed.

Today had been Viera's first real insight into what a Pillar did on Earth. It was 'Take Your Newbie Pillar to Work Day.' She'd come to be introduced to some of the government officials and begin to learn her way around. Though she hadn't said much, she'd learned a lot from what she'd seen and heard.

Juk stood and held out his hand. "It's been a real pleasure. Ever since they gave me the files last month, the idea of meeting you has been a dream. This is just amazing."

One of Betsy's eyebrows slowly rose. "I wish I could say the same."

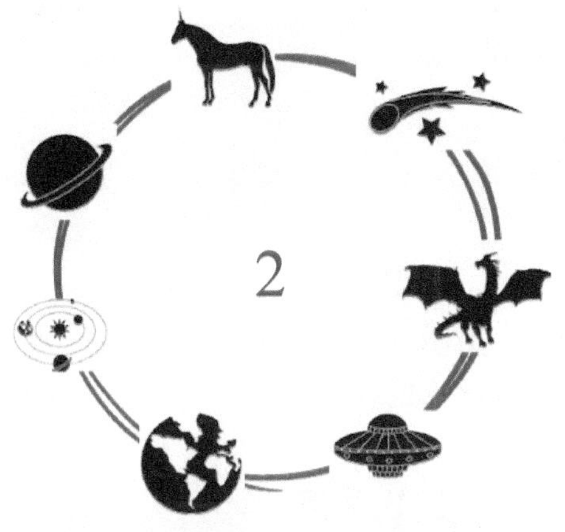

## 2

School's Out for ...

Viera

**"M**s. Kor, Ms. Kor, when will the bell ring? Ms. Kor!" Scout waved his hand in the air, dancing in his seat.

With a sigh, Viera rubbed her eyes. This day couldn't end fast enough. She raised an eyebrow at the boy. Of all the students in the classroom, he should know better. Very pointedly she drew her gaze from him to the clock on the wall, a digital clock that didn't take any work to read. The glowing red digits read two forty-three. Class would get out at a quarter past three.

"You tell me, excited boy: how long do we have?"

Next to him, Tiffany tilted her head. "We have a half-hour, Ms. Kor. Since we've cleaned the room and packed up, will you read us a story?"

Warmth suffused Viera. She was going to miss the young girl. Usually, Viera could track her students after they left her class, but this year was different. First of all, Tiffany was an alien, and more importantly, she was heading home. Thorn and Horax were taking Tiffany and her parents to Torville Station Number Six to find a transfer ship to their planet. The family had been on Earth for the last ten years, and they were excited to be heading home. Viera was happy to be traveling with a better understanding of what it meant to be on a spaceship with aliens.

The second reason she couldn't track the girl, or any of her students, was Viera was quitting her job as a teacher. Now that she was a Pillar, one of the very few magic-wielders on Earth, she felt she had a larger calling. She needed to focus on mastering her skills and be one of the six human go-betweens from the Earth governments and the different alien groups.

To be good at her new position, she also needed to learn about the diverse human cultures, as well as the myriad of aliens. She had a lot to learn. As her students would say: a lot of homework.

"Will you read, *If Mom Became an Octopus?*" Her smile brightened her face. Ever since she found out she was an octopus shifter, Tiffany had become obsessed with learning everything she could about the creatures. Earth octopi and what she came from weren't exactly the same, but she still got excited every time the lesson focused on the eight-legged cephalopods.

"Of course." The students all gathered on the reading rug and Viera sat in the reading chair. She took a moment to appreciate the simple act of reading a book to a group of young kids who enjoyed the story. She'd miss this. Sadness weighed heavy in her muscles as she read the book, then continued to read a few highlights and facts the book added at the end.

During the last few minutes of class, the students gathered their stuff and lined up to leave. This would be the last time she did this.

Viera realized the students blurred, and she blinked to clear her eyes. Over the weeks since spring break, one of the biggest lessons she'd focused on learning was controlling her sensing proficiency. Picking up the emotions, thoughts, and memories of the people around her could be overwhelming, fast. She released a bit of her hold to soak up her students' glee. Both the start of summer vacation and their excitement for starting third grade the next year.

Though Viera's future had become so much more than this classroom, with its motivational posters, and small chairs and tables, she'd miss it. She was about to embark on an amazing future and do spectacular things she'd never imagined possible. She, little old Viera Kor, was going to become an important person ... even if no one in the world knew it.

To her, teaching was one of the most important jobs out there. Helping children learn and grow both socially and intellectually. Walking away from this room ...

"Ms. Kor, are you okay?" Tiffany squeezed her hand.

Viera squatted down. "I am. I'm just going to miss this room and all you kids, that's all."

"Me too, Ms. Kor. Me too."

Out in the parking lot, Viera watched the last of her students walk off towards their home. Some students were picked up, but many lived close enough to walk. Scout and Tiffany rode together with Tiffany's parents, so Viera hadn't had a chance to see Thorn, much to her disappointment.

Tendrils of excitement and fear swirling within her, Viera turned to head back into the school. She was starting a new job. Would she be good enough? She was just an elementary teacher. Then there was the sadness of leaving the kids and other teachers she'd befriended. Over the years, she'd never gone as far as hanging out with any of her colleagues outside of school, but the other teachers and administrators were nice.

She sighed and slumped as she entered her room. "Well, Ms. Kor," she said to herself. "It's time to clean and pack up." The janitor had left her some boxes. Over the last week, she'd been packing up mementos she wanted to take with her, but this was it. Take it now or leave it forever.

Tears pricked her eyes as she wandered her room, finding small treasures she wasn't ready to part with.

"Are you really keeping all of those kids' projects?" A dubious voice brought her out of her classroom-wandering.

Turning, Viera saw the principal. She wore a smart navy-blue suit with a cream button-down shirt. In contrast, Viera wore jeans and a dark green blouse with a black cat on it hanging from a tree. It said across the bottom: *Hang in there!*

"I thought maybe I would, yes. Why, you don't think I should?"

The other woman huffed out a sound of disapproval. "Do you think you'll remember any of these kids in five years, Ms. Kor? Or even two years?"

Viera bit her bottom lip then put the sculptures the kids made of their favorite mythical creatures in her box. She told them they could take them home, but some decided to leave the figurines as a parting gift for her, some just forgot. As she wrapped each one in paper and secured them in her box, she said to the woman who'd intimidated her for years, "I may not remember which student made which one, but I'll remember the day they were made, the fun the students had, the creativity they put into each creature they created, and the love I had teaching them. The memories are worth savoring, even if some of the particular details are lost."

"You really are a dreamer, Viera, aren't you?" She sounded disappointed.

Not wanting to get into another one-sided discussion about how they differed, Viera squared her shoulders and stood a bit taller. "Did you want something?"

"Yes. We're holding a going away party. You were liked here ... by many. It started a half hour ago. There is pizza and ice cream, at least there was then. I believe there may even be a present for you. You're expected in the break room." After delivering her message, the principal spun on her heel and left.

*I wonder why she came and didn't ask someone else. Was she trying to be nice? Because if she was, she failed, brilliantly.*

With a final look around the room, Viera secured the last box. *Well, I guess that's everything. I can pack the car after I show my face at what is apparently my party ... that I wasn't invited to. Am I at all surprised?* She rolled her eyes as she walked down the hall to the soiree.

It's My Party ...

Viera

The elementary school wasn't large, though the hallways were wide. Viera's classroom was at the end of the second-grade wing. As she walked through the halls, empty and quiet with the start of summer, a sadness wrapped around her like a cloak, heavy and thick.

The walls were still covered in the students' artwork. Self-portraits with hopes and dreams, collages of scenes depicting images from books they'd read in class, and family trees with family members drawn on apples hanging from branches of an actual tree.

As she navigated to where teachers taught older students, some of the papers on the walls depicted math and science, others showed music or history. All along the side of the walls were random single shoes or gloves, a lost sock or a hat left behind from winter. All the items that students didn't want to drag home or think about again.

Most of this would end up in the lost and found or trash, depending on some system the school had in place.

The closer Viera got to the staff lounge, the more voices she heard. *I don't want to go in there. Too many questions I don't want to answer.*

Pulling up her metaphorical big girl undies, she squared her shoulders, and braced herself for the inevitable. After taking one final stabilizing breath, she walked with determination into the room, ready for any sort of cheer, or yell of 'surprise,' or general welcome from the other teachers she would no longer see on a daily basis. That was the thing that was making her wary, being the center of attention.

Entering the room, she saw a couple dozen people milling about with small plates overflowing with food. Some people sat at tables, but most stood as if waiting for the bell that told them they could leave. The swish of air behind her told her the doors were closed, but still, no one noticed her enter.

*What's worse, a yell of 'surprise' or everyone completely ignoring me?*

Viera grunted and headed over to the food. There were two trays, half picked over, with sliced cheddar, Swiss, and pepper jack cheeses. Next to the cheese were crackers, and then sliced sausage. The next tray had fruit: grapes, watermelon, cantaloupe, and strawberries. The final tray had store-bought bite sized-chocolate chip cookies—though most were gone—a plain-looking cookie, and a cake, with only two pieces left.

Pursing her lips, Viera selected two plates, and started to fill them. One with savory, and one with sweet. She started with one of the remaining pieces of cake. It was her party; she almost took them both.

"It said, 'Sorry to see you go, Ms. Kor, Good Luck!'" Gloria, one of the fourth-grade teachers said, sliding up next to her. "It was lovely. I have a picture. I'll text it to you. Where were you?"

Viera continued to fill her plate with the two types of cookies, then put that plate down to get some of the rest of the offerings. She figured she only had one trip before it was all gone. "I wasn't told about this shing-dig until about five minutes ago."

Gloria grunted. "Of course not. Why not tell the person of the hour about her own party. I should've predicted and texted you when you weren't here or, like, last week when the rest of us were told."

Frustration threatened to wash through Viera, but this was her last day, and she refused to let this place bring her down. "It's okay. I'm here now, and if I'd been here at the start, I'd probably have to talk in front of everyone."

Gloria smiled. "Probably."

They moved to one of the tables to sit. The cheese and crackers were a good start, and the fruit was fresh.

"Skipping the important part of your good-bye party and crashing it for the food?" Donald flopped in a chair next to Gloria and across from Viera. He taught band to all the grades. His bark was definitely worse than his bite.

"Yep, you know me." Viera winked at him.

He sat up, elbows on the table, and rested his chin on the back of his intertwined fingers. "You weren't told, were you? Our fearless leader, for whatever reason, wasn't going to tell you about this party?"

Viera's eyes narrowed. "Whose idea was it?"

He smiled wide. "Not telling, but I'm glad she was convinced to collect you. Now, Ms. Kor, tell me, where are you off to? I know you loved working with the kids, and they adored you. Why leave? In trouble with the law? Skipping town? Leaving the country? Marrying rich?" His eyebrows danced as his questions got more and more ludicrous. Or at least, to him they did.

*Well, I will be leaving the planet with my very rich girlfriend ... but I don't think that's what you're talking about.* She clenched her jaw to stop herself from smiling.

"No, nothing like that—"

"Don't you know? Viera here doesn't go more than fifteen minutes from our fair town. Leaving the state? That will never happen."

Viera sniffed in annoyance. "I'll have you know, I've taken the kids on field trips to Milwaukee *and*

Chicago. Both those cities are over an hour and a half away. Unless my math is very off, an hour and a half, and three hours are both more than fifteen minutes."

Viera indicated a free seat when she saw Ryan, another teacher, approaching them.

Gloria scoffed. "Field trips don't count."

Ryan, a third-grade teacher, sat down at their table. "If you're traveling on a bus with a bunch of elementary kids, it counts double."

"And *that's* why you're my favorite," Viera said, smiling at the other teacher. *I hope he ends up with most of my students.* "Now, as wonderful as all this is, most of the people have left since I've arrived and only you three even noticed me. All of you have my number; don't be strangers."

They all hugged, and Viera headed back to her classroom to gather her purse, keys, and last box.

After dreaming of teaching, going to school to be a teacher, and spending the last several years teaching, Viera never thought she wouldn't teach. Her heart ached for the end of this piece of her life. She knew ... she *knew* this was the right decision. It still hurt. Each step was heavier than the last as she made her way to the car.

*This is it. I'm leaving and I won't be a teacher anymore.*

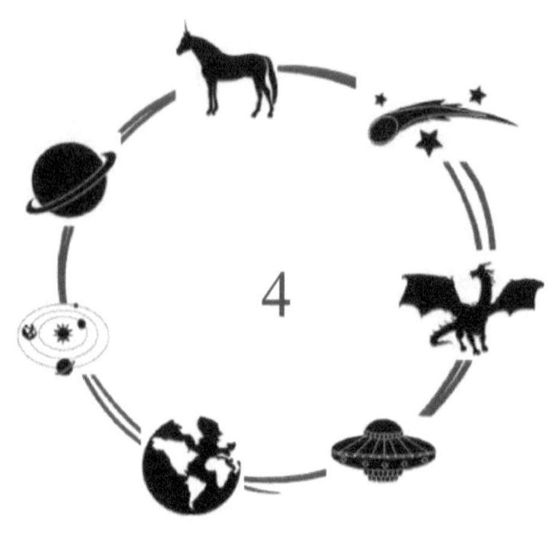

## Bye, And Thanks For All The Sushi

### Thorn

Thorn knew she had it easier than most elementary school kids' parents. It was the last day of school and Scout would be home in about an hour. He wasn't really the eight years he looked, not with her people's slow aging. He was really twenty-three. That didn't mean he acted twenty-three, though; he was very mature compared to the other eight-year-olds he played with, but he was still just a kid.

Unlike the other parents of the kids in his class, if she wanted to leave Scout home alone, she had no worries that he could care for himself. They had the electronic panel that produced food by request. She'd asked Juniper, one of the ship's technical experts, to add restrictions on the food types he could select. He could also entertain himself for an evening. She sometimes asked Horax, the ship's tactical officer and engineer, to watch Scout. He could do anything and loved the boy almost as much as she did.

Checking over the evacuation plans on a hand-held tablet, Thorn massaged her temples. When the krottel invaded her planet, Abritos, and her people were scattered, about a million ended up on Earth. Now that the Elders declared the Abritos needed to be given back, the overall turnover time was set for roughly two Earth years. As Commander and leader of her people, Thorn had a mission. She and the Pillars wanted to keep the Earthlings ignorant of aliens. That said, the chanzii planned on gradually evacuating, not wanting to make their exodus obvious.

Time was of the essence. Thorn clicked some symbols on her panel, and after a few moments,

Violet North's face popped up on her screen. The other woman had selected a petite blond human appearance with sea blue eyes. "Afternoon, Commander Firoza. To what do I owe the honor of your call?"

"I'm updating my spreadsheets. How many chanzii have left the planet? How has the evacuation been going in your area?"

Violet smiled, eyes darting to the left. "We've had just under thirty-thousand evacuate in the first wave. Many of our people have been itching to leave. Staying in an altered form has been rough."

Thorn rubbed her nose. "Shouldn't we be aiming for closer to fifty-thousand chanziian each month if we're hoping to evacuate a million of our people in twenty-four months?"

There was a gusty sigh. "Yes, but we need a place for the people to go."

Thorn's monitor beeped. She checked the name of the incoming call. "Violet, I'm going to bring Major Shifts into our conversation. I want his update as well, and hearing this directly will save me time."

Her face lit up at the honor of being invited into the call.

Thorn tapped her panel and the Major's stern turquoise face framed in flowing dark purple hair popped onto the screen. *I miss my natural shape!* His brilliant green eyes shone with concern. "Major Shifts, Commander Firoza here. I have Violet North on the line. She was updating me on the evacuation of Earth, but we can circle back to that after the Abritos update. I mean, we need a place for the chanzii to go so the planet is our highest priority."

His face scrunched up. "Well, ma'am, that's just it, we may need to change our timelines."

Anger spiked through Thorn. "Are the damn bugs refusing to leave? I swear I will round up the freaking Elders and drag them by their horns to make them force those creatures from our planet!" She could see red, she was so mad.

Major Shift's eyes widened as she ranted. His hands lifted and he shook his head. "Wait, no. That's not what I meant. We need to be careful, but I'm not sure if there are any bugs left on the planet. If the krottel are really all gone, we can start sending in crews to rebuild. Our timelines can be moved up, not back."

For a moment, Thorn was flabbergasted, unsure how to react.

Violet, who had been quiet up until then, giggled. "Apparently their evacuation strategy is as rapid as their invasion."

Thorn laughed, and she realized she sounded a bit manic. They were gone? The krottel had left their planet that fast? Could it really be that simple? Nothing with the freaking bugs was that easy. *I'll have to talk to Betsy about this ... it means Earth is probably in more danger ... but my people? We're going home!*

The three continued to discuss Abritos, the krottel, and evacuation. They decided to talk again once there'd been a better survey of the planet.

Once off the phone, Thorn sighed and leaned back. She'd heard Scout come home and head to his room during the call; school was finally out.

Thinking of school made her think of Viera. She missed Viera. She hadn't seen her in over a week. They'd both been busy—her with evacuation planning, Viera with all the work of finishing out the last days of her teaching.

*I wonder what she'd do if she came home and found me at her house?*

Back at her computer, she made another call.

"Commander Firoza, how can I help you?" A large, blue-scaled qynad—dragon to these silly Earthlings—faced her through the screen.

"Horax, could you come down and hang out with Scout? I'd like a night off. I'd leave him alone for the night, but Tiffany may be with him, and I don't think her parents like her without supervision."

The qynad's eyes danced with glee. "My pleasure. I've been looking for an excuse to get off this ship."

As soon as he'd transported down, Scout ran out from his room. "Horax! Can we play re'tast with Tiffany? We can go to the community center."

Horax nodded. "We sure can. Is Tiffany here?"

"Not yet. We can reprogram these tablets to teach Galactic Standard from English. Both Tiffany and Ms. Kor need them. I want to see if I can do it."

As the two hunkered down to work, Thorn contacted the ship for a transport to Viera's house. She knew the soon-to-be-retired teacher would still be at work if Scout had only just gotten home. Her girlfriend always had something to do after school, even on this last day of classes.

In Viera's house, Thorn headed to her kitchen. *What can I make her for dinner? She's probably had a long day. If she's had to deal with that principal ....* Thorn imagined the ways she could torture the manipulative bitch. There weren't many people she didn't like, but the principal of her son's school was near the top of the list, a few notches below the krottel.

There wasn't much in the fridge. Her mind spinning, she tried to piece together a meal but couldn't quite fit the pieces together. She found honey in the cupboard then turned to the panel on the wall. "I guess you'll be cooking tonight. Bottle of Port wine, while I wait."

The bottle appeared. She went to a cupboard and selected two periwinkle glasses. All her spoils in hand, Thorn went out to the living room to wait for Viera. She placed the glasses and wine on the table. Narrowing her eyes, she returned to the kitchen and found a bowl and filled it with a few pieces of ice. Viera's freezer made ice in the shape of orange slices, which Thorn always found intriguing.

Back in the living room, she sat on the couch and shut her eyes. *This is the first time I've relaxed in weeks.*

It felt like she'd only closed her eyes for a moment, but the sound of the key in the lock jolted her awake. It couldn't have been too long; the ice hadn't melted. Thorn stood to meet Viera at the door.

When the door opened, Viera gasped at the sight of Thorn. She dropped her bag as Thorn wrapped her in a hug, dipping her head down to capture Viera's mouth in a kiss. Viera slid her hands around Thorn's waist, holding on as if Thorn were a lifeline.

After too little time, Thorn pulled back. "Welcome home, Viera."

She groaned. "You're a sight for sore eyes. A balm on a long day." She smiled sheepishly. "Not that I'm not thrilled to see you—or baffled that you and Betsy can always get into my house whenever you want—but what are you doing here?"

"I missed you."

Viera let her head fall forward, her forehead resting on Thorn's chest. "I missed you, too." Her hands tightened on Thorn's hips. "It feels like it's been a lifetime. I'm very happy to see you ... and kiss you." She lifted her head, blue eyes gazing into Thorn's. "I'm hoping there's more?"

Thorn wrapped her arms around Viera and picked her up. Viera squealed. After kicking the front door closed, she carried the smaller woman to the couch and dropped her onto the cushions. Kneeling next to her, Thorn kissed her again, her hand exploring the treasures beneath Viera's shirt. "Oh, yes." She purred. "Much, much, more."

Viera's eyes crinkled at the side as she smiled mischievously. "But you're wearing too much clothing."

Thorn laughed, then stood, pulling Viera up with her. Feeling light-headed and addicted, she leaned down for another kiss before pulling Viera's shirt off. "Okay, you do the rest. I'm pouring some wine."

"I don't have wine."

With a snort, Thorn tilted her head to the table. "Then what's that?" She filled each glass with the bottle she'd uncorked earlier, to let it breathe.

Viera laughed. "Oh! Wine."

Thorn swirled the red liquid and sniffed the earthy scent before handing a glass to Viera. "You do know you have a panel in your kitchen that will grant all your culinary wishes, right?"

"Hmm? Yum," Viera said, seeming distracted. "Oh, I keep forgetting. Yes, the panel of wonders."

After sipping the wine, Thorn slipped out of her jeans and shirt, noticing Viera watched her every motion, tongue darting out as she licked her lips.

"One sip, then I'm mimicking that tongue of yours, licking *your* lips ... but maybe not the ones on your face."

Viera's face turned so red, Thorn thought she'd light on fire. Gently taking the glass from Viera, she placed them both on the table. She helped the other woman out of her clothes, then navigated her back to the couch, lying her down with a series of small kisses along her cheek and neck.

Once Viera laid back, her body flush from the wine, Thorn reached back for the bear-shaped honey bottle. Beneath her other hand, resting on

Viera's upper belly, she felt her lover tense. "What are you going to do with that?"

"You'll have to trust me."

Viera breathed shakily but didn't leap up from the couch and run for the hills.

Tipping the bear's head down, Thorn created a small bit of art on Viera's body. A wavy line starting at her neck. The path was small dots of the golden syrup that looped once around her right breast, with a larger drop at the top. A second drop went to the other nipple with the pebbled line continuing down, across her abs, with another circle around her belly button. It ended just above the juncture of her legs.

Thorn reached down and gently stroked between the folds of Viera's most private area. Her lover was hot, and wet, and obviously enjoying herself. "You seem to be liking my 'more,' Ms. Kor."

After a rough inhale of breath, and a sharp jerk of her head, she smiled. "It has promise, Commander Firoza."

Thorn continued to gently caress her, her finger tracing up and down between Viera's legs, while they spoke. "You seem to be getting ... a bit warm. You know, down here." She plunged a finger in

Viera's tight wet core, and the woman gasped, arching up. Her finger pumped in and out as she spoke. "I think we need to cool you off until I'm ready for your heat to come to a boil, my little fire cloud."

Viera just whimpered.

With her free hand, Thorn took a piece of ice, and replaced her finger with it. Viera gasped, then groaned as her hips rotated. "I think a second piece should fit in there while I clean all this honey off you. It's a perfect map of where my mouth should start and end, don't you think?"

After opening her mouth as if she wanted to answer, Viera simply licked her lips and nodded.

Thorn slipped a second piece of ice in. She could feel Viera tremble. Then Thorn knelt on the floor next to Viera and began licking and sucking the honey from the other woman's body. She didn't want any of the sticky substance to be left behind. She paid special attention to each breast, double checking with her hands once her mouth was done to make sure they were each perfectly un-sticky.

When Thorn finished with Viera's nipples, she was low enough to let her left hand wander to Viera's clit, drawing small circles and adding more pressure as she licked lower and lower. She could feel the coolness from where the ice had melted, and let her fingers trace to bring some of the cold up. When she finished the last of the honey, Viera screamed out her release, head thrown back, and body arched, pushing into Thorn's mouth.

Viera let her head fall to the side, gazing at Thorn. "I want my dessert before dinner, and you, Commander Firoza, are going to be my dessert. On your back ... now!"

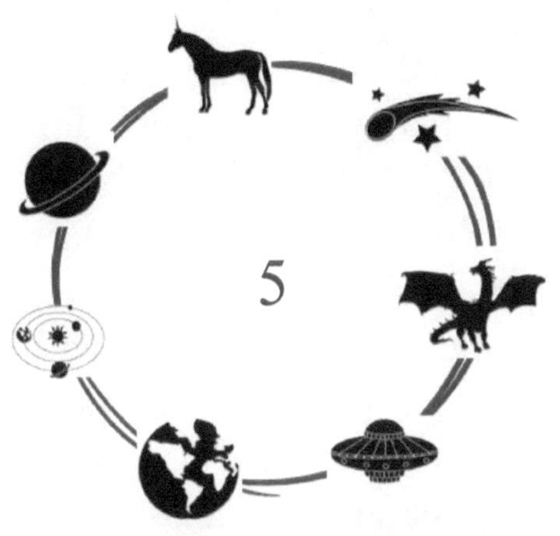

## Catching Up On Gossip

### Viera

The alarm buzzed and Viera groaned, not wanting to get up to have to deal with the day. The heat in her room, the warm body she rubbed against as she shifted to turn off her alarm, reminded her that she didn't have to wake up; school was out for the summer. Moreover, it was out for good.

Thorn's arm wrapped around her, possessively, dragging her back to mold against the other woman's front. Viera sighed in pleasure at how well they fit together. Her phone's buzzing on the side table, the sound her mind had translated into her alarm, echoed in the silent room. She reached over to check the display and silence it before it woke up Thorn.

*What the hell is my mother doing calling me at seven in the morning ... or at all?*

Though she didn't want to leave the bed, or Thorn's embrace, Viera had to take care of this before Mother called Betsy or worse, the police. After her disappearance during spring break, Viera had no idea what Mother would do if left with nothing but her imagination.

Viera set the phone down and twisted to give the sleeping Thorn a kiss on the cheek. She then wiggled out of bed, found a robe, and, after slipping it on, took her phone to the kitchen. Coffee was a necessity when dealing with family. She walked up to the panel. "One coffee, in one of my own mugs, if you please."

For the first few weeks she'd had the panel, it kept creating black mugs every time she requested tea or coffee. At first, Viera watched the news, worried there would be a story about a person or store missing goods. Then Horax had explained to her that the panel just made the thing it wanted from base elements in the areas. Despite not relying on thievery to get the mugs, Viera didn't need a collection of new black plateware. She finally learned the command so the panel would use her own stuff and not create more clutter.

Viera placed the coffee on the table, then added a pinch of sugar and a splash of milk. The panel could learn and create the perfect cup of liquid go-go juice for her, but she preferred to keep some of the steps under her control. She wasn't ready to give it all up ... not yet.

After her first few sips, she navigated to her mother's number and placed the call.

"Viera! You're alive. And available." Mother sounded frantic and a bit happy, with both emotions vying for top billing.

She didn't try to hide her exasperation. "It's seven in the morning here. You know we're an hour behind."

"But it's a weekday. Don't you have school?"

"Yesterday was the last day of classes. It's summer break. It was my first day to sleep in, Mother." Maybe some guilt would get her off the phone sooner.

"Oh, yay! That means you'll have some time to go on dates. No more Miss Busy-Pants."

*Or maybe not. I have got to put on my big girl panties and stand up to my mother. I have a beautiful woman—in my bed! Why would I even pretend to be anything but happy?*

"No, Mother. No dates."

"But, Viera, darling, I don't want you to be alone."

"Mother." She took a deep breath before her voice went any higher. She really didn't want to wake up Thorn. "Mother." Good, she sounded rational this time. "I don't need to be set up on dates. I'm fine with arranging my own. You don't know my type and the dates end up being flops. Please, just let me do—and be—my own person."

There was a pause and then Mother scoffed. "And what's wrong with the men I've set you up with? They're good men."

*Well, the problem is, they're men.* Viera rolled her eyes. *Fuck it! I'm tired of this shit.* "Well, Mother, to start with, I don't date men."

"I don't understand what you mean. Are you saying you're asexual? You don't date?"

*Just say yes ... just say yes.* Viera grimaced. No, she had to bite the bullet. "No, I'm saying I prefer to date other women. Actually, one woman in particular."

Her mother scoffed. "Well, that's just silly."

There was a muffled shuffling sound, and then Father's voice came over the line. He never spoke on the phone. Viera was glad she was sitting. "Viera? This is your father. Your, ah, aunt, you know, my sister? Well, she's married to a woman." There was a pause as if he were gathering his thoughts. "So, what I'm saying is ... I'm glad to hear you've found someone. Maybe we can meet her someday."

Viera had to gather her thoughts as well. *How did I never know this? Aunt Dotty is gay? I know I haven't seen her in ... God above, years. Father stopped talking about her when I was six? Maybe eight?*

"She came out to me and your grandparents when you were a young girl. None of us reacted well. Anyway, I'll send you her contact information. I mended that fence once I realized we'd been wrong. I'll talk with your mother. Get her to understand. You come and visit, okay? Bring ... bring your lady friend."

Viera blinked away moisture rising in her eyes. "Yeah, okay. I'll see what I can do."

He grunted and then hung up. Viera gaped at her phone. *What just happened?*

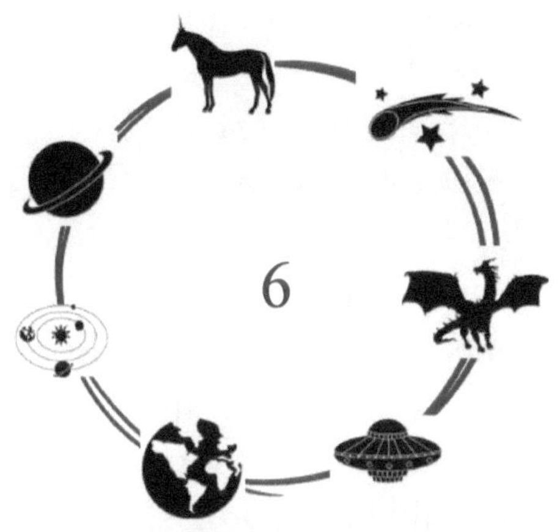

## Good Enough For Government Work

### Viera

Viera picked up her coffee, hands trembling in the aftermath of her boldness. The mug warmed her to her soul.

Thorn came down and, after getting her own coffee, joined her at the table. "Morning, fire cloud."

At first the chanziian term of endearment sounded weird, but now it tickled her. "Morning, my lovely sunshine."

Thorn sat and took her first sip. "Waking up with you is much nicer when you're there to wake up with."

Viera's smile faltered. "Yeah, my parents called. Mother wanted to start setting me up on dates again now that school is out. I told her to stop." Once she'd sipped her coffee, she put the mug down. "I told my parents I didn't need them to set me up with any more men ..." A small growl escaped Thorn, before she could respond, Viera continued. "I *told* them I could find *women* to date on my own. I even said I had someone in my life. They said they wanted us to visit."

A satisfied smile stretched across Thorn's face. "Well, maybe we can make that happen. Not this weekend—we're pretty busy with the trip coming up—but maybe once we're back. Ha! Meeting the parents." Thorn shook her head. "So, what are your plans for today?"

Leaning back, Viera sighed. "I'm going to drive over to Betsy's office and figure out what I've gotten myself into. I know my new job won't officially start until July, but I'd like to check in and see some of what she does—bridging the Earth governments and alien," Viera waved her hands around, "insanity."

With a chuckle, Thorn leaned over to gently kiss Viera. "I think you handle us aliens rather well."

Betsy worked downtown. Madison wasn't a huge city, but this area had been built on an isthmus between two lakes. The streets were a maze of one-way and two-way streets that often confused visitors. There were bikers and buses with their own lanes on some streets and sharing lanes with cars on others.

The heart of the city shared most of downtown with the flagship university of the state, the University of Wisconsin - Madison. Though the regular school year was out, there were still students out and about year-round.

Viera loved the general chaos of the city, though part of her missed living in a warmer climate. Madison suited her, but she wondered, once the chanzii were gone, with Betsy living in the area, if she'd have to relocate. *I really don't want to ... but I could. I didn't grow up here.*

Most of the street parking was metered, so, when confronted with the speedsters, and darting college students, Viera decided to navigate to a parking ramp.

The capital of the city sat in the center of the isthmus with roads leaving it in eight directions. There were two concentric circles of one-way streets that circumnavigated the capital that went in opposite directions. If Viera didn't know better, she'd think it was set up by the wizards as a focal point for some magical rites. One of the diagonal streets, State Street, angled from the capital towards campus. Traffic laws forbade cars to drive on it; only bikes, buses, and cabs were allowed. Betsy's office was above one of the shops on State Street.

After she'd parked, Viera walked the few blocks to the shop, then used the new code Betsy had given her for access to the second floor. There was a card she needed to use to get through a second security door and enter the offices.

Viera took a deep breath and wiped her hands on her pants. Nerves played within her like kids on a playground. *Am I really ready for this? Am I qualified? Is suddenly having magic enough to do this new job?* She thought back on the commute and what it took to get to the office. *God above, why didn't I just teleport? It would've been faster and easier than all this!*

There was a bright hallway with two doors on the street side and another door set into the interior wall of the building. Windows around the door looked into a conference room. The end of the hallway turned to the right. Viera assumed there were more doors, but she'd get the tour later, or she'd poke around on her own. She recalled Betsy's directions.

*'Once you get to the office, knock on the second door on the left. You could just come in, but if I'm really busy, I may accidentally blast you.' Betsy laughed at her own joke, and they quickly ended their call.*

Smirking at the memory, Viera knocked. She loved Betsy's sense of humor ... at least she thought her friend had been joking.

"Come in, Viera. You're late." Betsy's voice was curt, but she ruined any harshness by chuckling at the end.

*Okay, this is it. I can do it. Betsy has confidence in me ... I should, too.*

She plastered a smile on and opened the door. "How can I be late? We didn't set a time."

"You're a teacher. I thought you'd be here by seven-fifteen, or some crazy time like that."

The office was large, but you couldn't tell with all the filing cabinets Viera could almost hear groaning under the weight of everything they held. The windows that faced the street were blocked by bins filled with papers in disarray. Her friend's desk had more stacks surrounding her laptop and large monitor. There were two chairs on the door side of the desk, but only one was cleared off. The avocado green seat and metal arms reminded Viera of images of offices from the fifties.

"You and Mother both. I'm no longer a teacher, and eight-thirty is early enough." She sat in the chair and was pleasantly surprised at how sturdy it was.

"You spoke with your mother this morning?" One of her brows rose, asking for more details.

"And Father. They know I'm dating a woman and hopefully will stop trying to set me up."

Betsy whooped. "About time."

"Okay, can we focus?" Viera felt her face warm. "What have I gotten myself into?"

"One sec." Betsy started typing on her computer. Then she adjusted the monitor so Viera could see it. There was a small camera sitting on the top of the screen. She saw five boxes appear. She recognized the other Pillars of Earth—the magic wielders, the wizards.

Marco took up the upper left corner, his boyish face all smiles. Behind him, he'd set a scene of a tropical beach. *Or is he on a tropical beach? Anything is possible with these people.* Next to his image, Ania's older face beamed at her. Knowing how the Pillars aged, Viera couldn't fathom what it took to cause one of them to get laugh lines around their eyes and to start to gray. She finally met the Australian woman a couple of weeks ago. Her fiery red curls bounced near her shoulders and her pale green eyes shone.

On the bottom row, Zuza sat in his office in London amongst his books. His crystal blue eyes, a contrast from all the wood and leather tomes. Finally, Kafi sat back in the last box. Like Marco, his younger face belying his aged wisdom.

"Okay, everyone," Betsy said, her mouth twitching to hold back a smile. "Viera is *finally* here to learn about what we do."

*Yep, totally ready. That's me. Do I need to take notes?* She looked at the piles of paper and decided any notes would be lost in the crazy that was this office. She could always ask Betsy if need be.

Ania's smile widened. "You do know it's the middle of the night here, don't you? I should be in bed right now, like a good old lady."

Marco snorted. "As if, Ania. You're probably just starting your day right now, midnight or not!"

The older woman laughed. "Okay, fine. Well, think of poor Kafi, he's probably only just woke!"

Zuza shook his head. "Enough. Poor girl needs to learn what we do."

Leaning forward, Kafi's warm voice flowed over the computer, his African accent filling the room. "Most of our job is ensuring the general population doesn't freak out. Our people don't know about magic, but I'm sure they will one day. So, in a nutshell, our current job is to find anything that will give up the secret and hide it, and one day, when the secret comes out, help with the freak out."

Viera bit her lip. "That second half sounds awful." *God above, please don't let that happen on my watch!*

Zuza snorted. "You are correct. We can just hope that we can keep aliens from letting our people know about themselves or from magic from becoming known to the public."

"Oh! Aliens. I didn't think about that." Viera rubbed her face. "If the aliens become known, magic will surely follow. It'll be the Big Bang of massive amounts of work. No wonder you all wanted me to join your crew." Smiles and laughter followed her words. "My one other question is, you all live all over the world, but Betsy and I are both here. Is that okay?"

There were some shrugs and eye shifts, then Ania sighed. "It doesn't really matter where we're located. The work is what matters. Betsy has been working with the chanzii and a lot of her day-to-day responsibilities have been piling up. Having you there to learn from her and help will be fine. Once you have your own duties, having you both in the same office won't matter. When we need to meet, we teleport. We have the technology, even without the chanzii around."

Marco winked. "Do you feel like you're ready to start your job?"

Eyes widening, Viera slowly shook her head. "Not even a little."

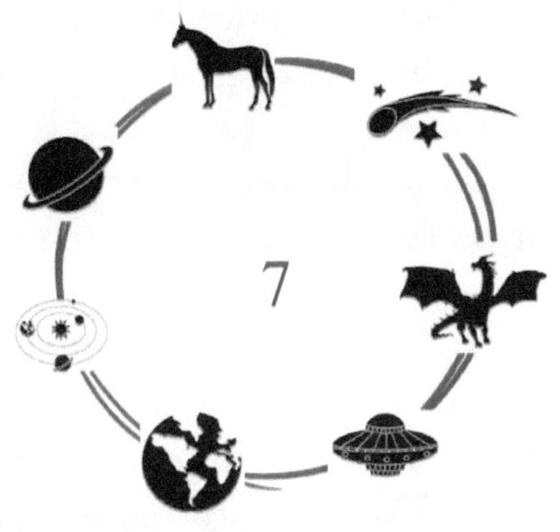

# 7

## Sky's Clear - Until They're Not

### Betsy

It didn't take long for the full complement of Pillars to finish their discussion and end their call. Everyone liked Viera. Having another person to help, increasing their numbers by twenty percent, no one was going to be upset by that.

"Are you freaking out yet?" Betsy rose to get Viera a mug of coffee. Her friend had sat still during most of the meeting, a smile plastered on her face. Even without a sensing proficiency, she knew Viera was nervous.

"Yes? No? I mean, that call gave me an idea what the job is, but I really don't know what you do, besides make a huge mess in here." She took the coffee and drank deeply. "God! This is good."

"Well, bring it with. Let me show you around." Outside her office, she pointed to the right. "The first door leads into a janitorial closet. The cleaners come to vacuum the main hallway and conference room. I don't let anyone in my office. We'd deny access to the level if we could, but the owners of this building don't allow that." *Maybe if I let them in, they'd see all my stacks of paper as recycling, and it'd cut my workload down.* She smiled at her thought and waved her hand to the left.

As she spoke, Viera nodded, taking it all in. They turned to walk. "Across the way is a huge conference room. We sometimes use it for our group meetings, though we have other options as well." At the end of the hall, the corridor turned right, hugging the large group space. "There are three doors along this hallway. The first is the restroom. Then a kitchen. And finally, at the end of the hall, is a second office I'd been debating using for a storage unit for my piles of paper. I may still do that, and let you deal with all the crap ... I mean *very important documents.*"

Viera chuckled, but it sounded more like a nervous laugh.

Since Viera hadn't planned to start working today, they did a quick look into each space, then headed back to Betsy's office. "That's it for today, unless you want—" A ping on her computer interrupted her. "Hold that thought, let's see where this goes." Opening up the communication app, she connected with the chanzii ship. "Horax, this is Pillar Doeth. I have Pillar Kor sitting in with me, if it's private."

Horax's deep baritone voice rumbled through her tiny laptop. "Nothing private, Pillar Doeth. The long-range sensors have picked up a ship. We believe it's krottel. There's no immediate indication it's heading this way, but I wanted you to know."

Annoyance and dread fought within Betsy. Despite her emotions, she kept her voice calm. "Thank you Horax. I know the chanzii ship is heading off to Torville Station Number Six on Monday, but would you be able to take me and a few others out to check that before you leave?"

His large blue qynad head, so like the dragons of legend, slowly nodded. "If we head out today, we should have the ship back, ready to prep for the ride by tomorrow. It'll be tight, but I can make it work. I'd need approval from Flower Prancer or Commander Firoza."

"Thanks, old friend." She signed off and prepared for another call, one she was less happy to make. Before she dialed, she turned to Viera. "Okay, that was the easy part. Next, we call the Earth authorities. I don't need their approval, but they need to know what's going on. I'll have to submit paperwork as well."

Viera's mouth twitched. "Are you calling that asshole? Juk Purple... wait, what was his name? Juk Asskisser?"

Betsy laughed. *I'm going to love working with Viera!* "Juk Hopkins." She resisted rolling her eyes like a teenager as she picked up the phone and dialed his number directly. The ability to call into an office of that government building shouldn't be possible, but age had its privileges.

"Juk Hopkins, how can I help you?"

"Hiya, Juk, Ms. Doeth here."

"Betsy ... ah, Ms. Doeth. How did you get through to me without contacting our operator?"

Betsy huffed out a laugh and waited. She figured his brain would catch up before too long; he did end up as her handler after all.

"Er, I mean, it's nice hearing from you. How can I help you this fine Friday? At least, I assume it's fine where you are ... I mean, I don't even know where you're located. Are you in D.C. like us? I mean, you don't have to divulge that, I was just. Gah! Can I start over?"

Viera's hands were over her mouth holding in a laugh. The kid's nerves were taking over worse than any of her other contacts. She didn't want to get a third person, but this kid was awful. "Juk, I'm just calling because a krottel ship was picked up on long-range sensors."

There was a small gasp. "Do we need to ... I mean, I'll have our people focus our searches. We haven't picked anything up."

Betsy massaged her temples. This kid was going to give her a migraine. "I'm going to take the chanzii ship out to the edge of our system to see if we can get a better idea of what's going on. No guarantees. They are leaving Monday for Torville Station

Number Six, so this will be a quick mission. I'll include any findings in my report. I just wanted to let you know what was going on."

"Um..."

"Good-bye Juk."

"Yeah, okay. Thanks, Ms. Doeth."

Betsy hung up before he could say more. She leaned back in her chair. "I think you should sit this one out. I don't think it'll be interesting. Go home, relax, pack, and prepare for the trip."

Viera slouched but didn't argue. "Okay. I guess that makes sense."

"It does. You just ended a big part of your life. You need some time to reflect before jetting off into space. Now, go, take some time to decompress."

Though Viera didn't look happy, she squared her shoulders and gave a quick nod. Then she stood and walked out of the office with a wave good-bye.

Once Betsy heard the main door shut, she picked up her phone and dialed Thorn. "Betsy, I didn't expect to hear from you. How can I help you?"

"Hi, Thorn. There is a situation. I'm not sure if you've been filled in, but I need use of the Ziner to check out a situation Horax found on the radar. Could I get your approval, and could you join us?"

There was a moment's pause then a muffling sound. "Miracle Max, get off the curtains. Inigo Montoya, so help me, you mangy ven, get down. Be like Buttercup and Westley; they know how to behave!" Thorn's voice came back stronger. "Sorry about that. These babies are learning to fly, and I am going crazy. I'm starting to wonder if they're half phoenix."

Betsy laughed. "Your pups are adorable, and you know it."

"Do you want one?" The hope in Thorn's voice made Betsy smile.

"They can't leave their mom for another few months; ask me then. Though, you should ask Viera first. If you give away her precious Fezzik, she may skin you alive."

Thorn grumbled. "She does love that annoying pup." She sighed. "I really need to get everyone here organized for the trip on Monday. Between Scout and Tiffany's family, who've been living in the ocean for years, it's more work than I like to think about. They want to leave, but don't want to be away from the salt water for that long. We keep having discussions about options. They've brought up *Star Trek IV* over and over."

This made Betsy laugh. "Are they looking for nuclear 'wessles?'"

"Exactly!" Thorn chuckled. "I had to watch the movie to figure out what they meant. Then I had to explain that filling a part of the ship with ocean water for a four-day trip when they could stay in human form indefinitely was ridiculous."

Betsy slumped. "Does this mean my request is denied?"

"No," Thorn said. "Just because I can't go, doesn't mean the ship isn't available. Why don't you call in Violet? You know her, right? Maybe Flower Prancer will want to go." There was a pause, and Betsy heard typing. "I'll make some calls. The ship will be ready to leave in an hour."

Betsy smiled at the room at large. She'd worked with Violet and liked the spunkier chanzii. "Thanks, Thorn. I'll contact Horax for the transport."

The bridge of the Ziner, the chanzii ship, was spacious. Even with two qynads, there was room to move around, though they did take up a quarter of the space. Betsy sat in an alcove area, out of the way of the crew, with a small rectangular table and four chairs, all bolted to the floor.

Next to her, Juniper, one of the engineers, sat with a wide smile on her face. Her curly dark purple hair flowed halfway down her back. "I know I'm supposed to be in engineering, but this is such a short trip, I can be just as helpful here. My second is down there in case anything needs immediate care."

Standing next to the table, Flower Prancer, with his violet eyes, glared disapprovingly at both of them. "Ensign Snow, if your place is in the belly of this beast, shouldn't you be down there?"

Juniper trembled at the Elder's attention. "Yes, sir." She slowly slid from her chair and slunk off.

Betsy narrowed her eyes at the yonat. On Earth, unicorns were supposed to be nice, friendly even—especially the ones with rainbow hair. This one was anything but. "You know, you aren't her captain, or even her supervisor. She was given leave to work from the bridge for this journey. You just undermined the command structure for no other reason than to strut your importance. When she gets in trouble for not being where she's supposed to be, I'm going to make sure they know it's your fault, and not hers."

He gazed down his very long nose at her. "If this was her assigned location, why didn't she just tell me, Pillar Doeth?"

She sneered. *Why am I even trying to socialize him?* "Because, Elder Flower Prancer, she was intimidated by you and didn't feel comfortable contradicting what you said."

He scoffed and they both went back to observing the crew prepare for the short flight.

While she watched, Violet, one of the chanzii leaders, entered the bridge from the lift and walked to the captain's chair, a huge smile on her face. "Crew, I know I don't often visit the ship, but I am proud and excited to lead you on today's mission. I am also thrilled to welcome Elder Flower Prancer and Piller Doeth to the bridge." She turned to them. "We are honored to have you join us today."

Everyone on the bridge turned and smiled at them.

Violet turned back to the screen. "We'll take the short jump to Pluto and send out a message. Then we'll wait for four hours, enough time for any ship to respond. After that, we'll consult with Elder Flower Prancer and Pillar Doeth before returning to planet Earth."

The crew applauded and everyone went back to prepping the ship for departure.

Once the ship left Earth's orbit, Violet came over to personally welcome Betsy and Flower Prancer to her ship. "I'm thrilled and honored to have two such distinguished passengers."

Flower Prancer bowed his head. "I am going to go below for a few minutes. Let me know when we reach our destination. I would like to oversee the dispatch of the message."

"Of course, honored Elder."

He shot Betsy a look, as if to say, "*See? This is how you ought to address me.*" Then he turned and sauntered from the bridge. Once he was gone, Horax snorted. "You two should go into the fighting box and battle it out. The fight would be epic. You'd make enough money to retire."

Betsy shook her head. "I have enough money to retire. I don't work for the pay. I do it because I love what I do."

Violet snorted, then covered her face with her hands. "Sorry."

"Oh, no, I was hoping to make someone laugh."

The two smiled, and an awkward silence followed. Finally Betsy shook her head. *When was the last time I was tongue-tied around someone? Quick, think of something to say!* "Why haven't we worked together before? You're located in the U.S.? Right? Seattle, Washington?"

"I am. And I don't know why we've never worked together; it seems like such a waste. We should rectify that, don't you think? Maybe discuss it over dinner sometime?" A slow smile crossed the other woman's face and there was a challenge in her eyes.

Betsy face heated. *For fuck's sake, I'm blushing. I don't blush. What is wrong with me?* "Sounds good. I'll have my people call your people."

Violate winked. "Mission first, dinner second—a plan!" She spun on her heel and strode back to her seat.

Lost in her thoughts about a date she didn't know *could* happen, she wasn't prepared when Horax bellowed, "We're here!"

She stood as the yonat returned to the bridge.

Horax tapped on the panel in front of him before turning to the crew. "The ship is definitely a krottel ship, but I still can't get a lock on their final heading."

Betsy considered his report. "I'd still like more information about what they're doing and where they're going."

Flower Prancer cleared his throat. "Are we ready to send a message?"

Horax waved him on.

"Krottel ship, this is Elder Flower Prancer. I am requesting information on your final destination. Planet Earth was restricted to you and your kind. Please send your answer post haste."

Their relative distance from the other ship meant their message should take no more than an hour to reach them, probably much less time. The reply should be to them in, likewise, an hour or less.

Betsy spent part of the time they waited showing Violet and Horax how to play poker. They'd seen Earth cards before and knew about gambling, but poker was new to them. Horax was particularly good. Generally, Betsy was a shark at the game, but she kept on being distracted by the enchanting acting captain of the Ziner.

After four hours, when no response came, they dropped a node into the vicinity that would amplify any message or signal from another ship and send it on to Earth.

Frustrated, Betsy's jaw clenched, and she shut her eyes to think about the reasons for the ship to be this close to Earth. She'd tried to distract herself with cards and flirting. *Gah! Me, flirt? No one would believe it.* All around her, the crew's faces were somber and tight with their apprehension as they turned the ship and headed back to Earth.

As they flew home, Betsy got out her laptop and began her report for Juk. She knew the government official would see this as a win for 'not worrying.' *The problem is, if there's nothing to be concerned about, then why am I so worried?*

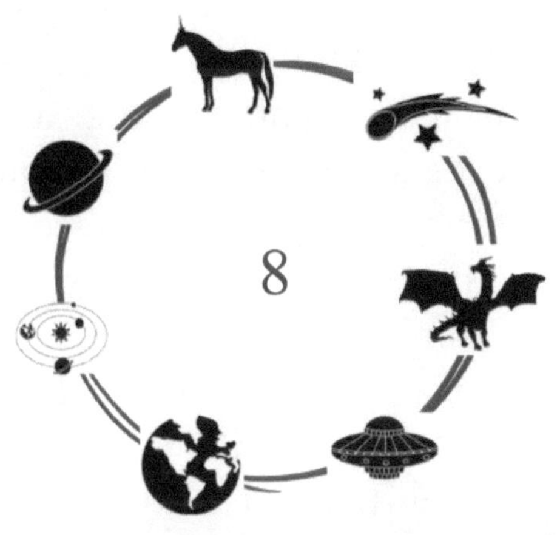

## Where's the App For That?

### Viera

Viera woke early Monday and double checked that all her stuff was packed. She had called her parents one more time over the weekend to tell them she'd be going back to that cabin up north and wouldn't have access to a wireless network. She'd call when she returned.

*I just hope they don't try Betsy while we're away. She's coming with this time.*

After one last circuit around the house to make sure all the electronics were off, Viera knew she'd put her departure off as long as she could. She tapped the panel. "Viera Kor, ready to leave—"

Before she could list what she wanted to bring, her house melted around her like a watercolor painting, and she suddenly stood in a quiet, clean, and spartan room. It had a bed, dresser, a window with stars on the other side, and three doors. Her body tingled from the transport.

Around her on the floor were all her bags.

Viera began at the window. She pressed her nose to the cool—but not cold—surface, but no matter how far out she looked, she could only see Earth. She could see the edges of the sun and most of the moon. That tickled her to her toes.

*Fuck! I'm in space again!* Chills ran up and down her body.

Spinning, she went to the first door on the left. A small bathroom with a shower. Peeking in, she saw the controls for the magical soak. Now that she was off Earth and its thick blanket of magic, she'd need to soak daily. Just seeing the yellow button made her relax.

The second door opened up to a closet. Inside she found ... *for fuck's sake!* She found Gandalf's walking stick. "Aren't you supposed to be back on

Earth in Betsy's house, safe and secure? What are you doing here? I'll have to find her and figure out what to do with you, you wooden menace!"

The third door, by elimination, headed out into the corridor. She knew she should unpack, but she decided to figure out where she'd been dropped on the ship and if she was needed for anything.

The hall was light blue and nondescript. The far wall had a panel, much like the one in her kitchen. She approached and said, "Can you show me where Scout is?"

Viera knew that Thorn, Flower Prancer, Horax, and even Betsy would all be on the ship. In all likelihood, they'd all be busy. Scout would know where everyone was, what they were doing, and who could be interrupted. The kid knew everything. If she could find him, he could provide all the information she needed or wanted.

Lights lit up along the floor in a wave, indicating the direction she needed to walk. As she sauntered down the hallway, the lights behind her went out and new lights began their dance in front of her. At one point they indicated a lift that brought her to a new floor, with the correct level pre-selected. By the time she arrived at the door, it occurred to her that she could've just called Scout and he'd have come to her room to show her around.

Laughing at herself, she knocked on the door. Tiffany answered. "Ms. Kor! Oh, my, what are you doing here?" The girl's face reddened as if embarrassed to see her teacher outside of school ... or maybe on the spaceship.

Before Viera could answer, Scout's voice floated to her. "Ms. Kor! You found us. Wanna play Candy Land with us?"

Viera relaxed. "I'd love to."

Scout's head appeared in the doorway. "Tiffany has a bunch of games. We're practicing chanziian while we play. You want to learn my native language, too, right?"

She nodded at the boy's exuberance. "I do. I'd love to join you in both the games and the language lessons."

In the room, a bigger family set of rooms, with a living space, small dining room table, and several doors, sat Juniper. She smiled at Viera. "I decided to spend some time getting to know Tiffany."

"Sounds good to me." Viera took her place to the other woman's left. They started a new game.

Scout patiently explained colors and numbers as they flipped over the cards. On her turn, Viera always tried to repeat the colors back. "I'm going to hold off on the numbers for now and just focus on colors. Two tsu-za."

Everyone at the table beamed at her as she moved her piece forward two red spots. Apparently Tiffany had mastered the colors already.

When it got to her turn again, she drew red again. She held out her hand to forgo any help. "One su-za."

Juniper opened up her mouth to say something, but both Tiffany and Scout laughed. Finally Scout said, "You said a horse, Ms. Kor, not one red."

Her brow furrowed. "A horse? I thought I said the same thing."

He shook his head. "You said *su*-za, not *tsu*-za." The two words he said sounded almost identical. She'd have to see the words written down.

Smiling at him, she nodded. "Okay."

The remainder of the game involved color identification. She was right about fifty percent of the time.

*If only I knew what I was doing wrong! Why isn't there an app for this?*

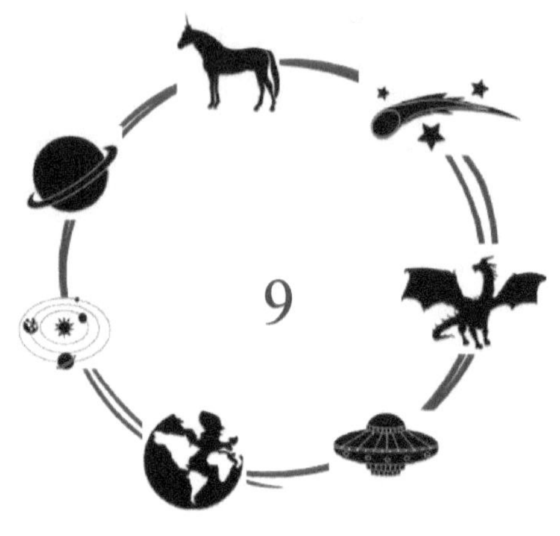

# 9

## Your Box Or Mine?

### Viera

Viera stretched, yawned, and opened her eyes. She knew with the gizmos and dumaflaches, there was no way she could feel the movement of the ship, but her low-grade nausea told another story. Her arms trembled as she pushed herself up. "God above, I need to soak in magic. Is this trip worse than the last one?" she mumbled to herself. "Maybe it's because I use magic."

There was no one to answer her, but she couldn't think of any other reason for the way she felt. *I should see about adopting one of the ven, then when I talk to myself, I'd really be talking to Fezzik or one of the others ... but probably him.* Viera's head pounded. After a day of playing games with Juniper, Scout, and Tiffany, her head was full of very few chanzii words, and she hoped to hang on to the little she had. She worried every pound was a word lost.

Chanting the colors in chanziian, or at least what she hoped were the colors, Viera trudged to the closet and pulled open the door. Her bags were piled in the bottom, blocked by the damn walking stick. When she'd returned to her room the night before, she'd stuffed her bags away to get them out of her way but didn't feel like doing much more for the two-night flight.

With a sigh, she yanked her bag out and flopped it on the bed, unzipping the large bag.. She selected the top pair of jeans and clean panties, then stood to grab one of the tops that the ship's crew had stocked in the closet. She loved the doublet tops and thick black belts. They were comfortable and nothing like what she wore back home. She didn't know what the different colors meant, but since no one had criticized her, and the clothes were in her closet, she didn't care. In the center, she found a brilliant purple top for the day.

With clothes draped over her arm, she continued her trek to the bathroom. Viera stripped and stepped into the small washing area. In the shower, she quickly pressed the blue button and a wave traveled over her body, giving her a tingling sensation. Despite all the upgrades of living in an alien world, she still wasn't sure what she felt about waterless cleaning. Like the last time on the ship, she smelled her armpits, impressed again at how well the alien shower cleaned, and felt her skin and hair. Everything seemed to be in order.

*It's a marvel what these people must save on shower products!*

Satisfied, she tapped the yellow button. A second invisible wave, this time a soak of magic, traveled down her body. The end result was more substantial, making Viera feel grounded ... ironic while flying in a spaceship. Remembering the warning of a few months back, she did a double soak. A lesson with Flower Prancer wasn't on her schedule, but that didn't mean the cantankerous Elder hadn't planned one on his own.

The sensation of the shower water splashing down over her face in the morning often made her feel awake and ready to face a room full of eight-year-olds. She'd take a leisurely fifteen-minute shower to wake up and center herself for the day. Here on the ship it took less than five minutes to get clean and soak in magic. Viera pulled on clothes, just as tired as when she pushed herself up and out of her warm bed, when a yawn cracked her face.

*Time to find food ... and coffee! Lots and lots of caffeine.*

While Tiffany and her family were located on a different level, Betsy and Thorn were both on this level, as was Scout. Thorn and Scout didn't have a family unit; the trip wasn't long enough, and Scout liked a bit of freedom. Also, as the ship's captain, Thorn was in and out at all hours. Scout could sleep better without interruptions in his own separate room. Their rooms were next door to each other.

As it went, Viera was assigned a room on the other side of Scout's. Just as she stepped out, she heard him laughing, a feat considering the soundproofing installed in the walls and doors of the Ziner. Curious, she knocked on his door ... well, typed the command to ring his bell on the pad to the right of his door. It took a moment for his door to open, and then an avalanche of baby ven were atop her. As they all focused on her, Buttercup and Westley climbing her legs, Inigo perched on her shoulder, Fezzik on her head, and ... "Where is Miracle Max?"

Scout's laughter filled the hallway. "Ms. Kor, you're covered in ven; it's a look! You could walk down the runway at a fashion show, make a new statement. The ven statement!" He fell over laughing. Just then Miracle Max flew out the door and down the hallway followed by Beaver, the baby ven's mom. She was much bigger than the pint-sized moth-like creatures, with big dark eyes, and long antenna, and ready to catch her escapee.

Viera tried to turn but feared for the babies atop her.

Thorn came out of her room and rolled her eyes. "For goodness sake, Scout, can't you control those things? They're all over Viera. Look at her, she's acting like a statue. As if, because they're on her, she can't move. Like *they're* the boss."

Viera pet Fezzik; he was so soft. A low rumble came from his belly. "But, Thorn, they're so happy."

"You know what? You and Scout can deal with this. I have to get to the bridge." Her face softened. "Are you free tonight for dinner? I missed you last night. I was kind of hoping you'd share my box ... er, my room."

Viera shifted her gaze to Scout when Thorn said 'box,' but the boy had taken off down the hall after the missing ven.

Thorn stepped up to her and lifted Viera's chin for a kiss. "Is that a yes? Tonight? I'd like to be around you when we go through the GPS so you're not alone, and then, you know, watch over you until we both wake up." Her grin was devious.

Heat made Viera feel alive and excited way too early. Despite the baby ven using her as their play structure, she placed her hands on Thorn's hips and smiled. "That all sounds great, though not soon enough."

Thorn leaned down for one more kiss before turning on her heel to head for the lift. "Oh! And no ven!"

Viera laughed as Scout ran up. "Okay, let's get them all back in the room. Have you eaten?"

"Nope. I was about to head off to find food."

He slumped. "Thank goodness. I'm starving." He darted into his room and the sound of hard ven food hitting bowls echoed out. As quickly as they attacked her, the baby ven were gone.

She laughed. "Traitors. You only want food!"

Scout darted out, shutting his door. "Do you blame them? That's all I want, too."

They found Tiffany sitting alone at a table. They both sat and, after deciding what they wanted, Scout headed to the kitchen to pick up their order.

Viera considered the girl. "Why are you here alone?"

Tiffany shrugged. "My parents said they're on ..." Her forehead wrinkled as she thought. "They said a thing where they don't eat because they're mad at Scout's mom."

"A hunger strike?"

The girl's face scrunched up even more. "Maybe? I'm not sure."

Viera huffed in frustration. "Does anyone know that they're not eating because they're upset?"

"They said their absence would speak volumes. And, well, I guess it did since you noticed."

With a shake of her head, Viera thought about what she'd do with the information, if anything. *Three days won't kill the parents, and their passive-aggressive strike is a bit obnoxious. It isn't like anything can be changed mid-flight. Save me from adults acting less mature than my students.* "I guess I did notice, but mostly because I care for you." She reached over to squeeze Tiffany's hand. "I don't think I'm the person they wanted to notice."

Before Scout got back, Betsy arrived. She sat at their table next to Tiffany and across from Viera. She already had a plate with bacon, eggs, and toast. "Morning, everyone. I hope you all slept well."

Tiffany shrugged. "I did, but I miss the water. We don't even get water to shower with. It's so weird. I hope it's different at the space station."

Betsy gazed at the two of them then took a sip of coffee. "I didn't see you yesterday, Viera. I thought maybe you missed the ship."

Juniper took the seat on the other side of Betsy as Viera said, "I found the kids and started playing games with them. I learned some of the chanziian colors." One of Betsy's eyebrows rose. Viera sighed. "Like my top, it is su-nor, one of my favorite colors."

As she finished her example, Scout put down their plates with a loud snort. Her coffee splashed out a bit, and she sighed. Picking up the mug, she took a sip. She really needed liquid ambrosia this morning. Betsy's eyes danced and Juniper giggled softly. "Okay, what did I say wrong?"

Juniper's warm eyes crinkled at the side. "Su-nor is coffee; tsu-nor is purple. We can go over all of this more slowly if you'd like, later on. I've set up a tablet for you, so you can practice with seeing the words. I think it'll help. Though, you'll need to learn the alphabet first, which isn't easy either."

Scout sat sideways in his chair, facing her. After Viera took another drink of her coffee, she placed the mug well away from the edge of the table, or the boy, who still seemed animated from playing with the ven.

Viera turned to Betsy. "So, we didn't see each other, but a certain stick is in my closet. I don't know how or why, but it appeared when I checked yesterday and again this morning."

Betsy ran her fingers through her hair, front to back. "Well, hell. That thing must be attracted to your magic, and when you moved too far away, it followed, like a good pup. I guess we'll have to give in to inevitability. Maybe if you start carrying it around it will calm your magic down and help you to focus."

Viera's eyebrows shot up. "You think so?"

"Maybe."

Scout asked, "What stick?"

Viera shot Betsy a look, but she nodded. "If you're going to be carrying it around, people will find out anyway."

"Gandalf's old walking stick."

Scout's jaw dropped before he swung his hands out in disbelief. His left hand flew over the table and knocked over her coffee—her salvation, her ambrosia. It flew at Tiffany, scalding hot coffee hitting her in the chin and arm.

Her eyes widened, just as Viera yelped, "No!" Both hands up in a double stop sign position, as if that would stop anything.

*Oh my God, I have to fix this. The poor girl is going to get a burn, maybe even blister. She's had a hard enough life; she doesn't need that.* Viera faced Betsy, "What do we do?"

It suddenly sunk in, all the sounds from the room had stopped. No one moved, nothing shifted, it didn't look like anyone breathed. The coffee had just reached its target, the red of the burn barely beginning.

*What the hell? Did I stop time?* Looking around the room, everything ... everyone looked like statues. *How long can I hold this?*

Viera stood, slowly circling the table. She wanted to move Tiffany away from the coffee, but the damage was done. *God above, if I can stop time, why can't I do more?* She closed her eyes and thought as hard as she could—*undo undo undo undo!*

When she opened her eyes, everything in the room looked exactly the same. *What the fuck is the point of stopping time if I can't fix this? Is there a way to undo this damage?*

Her path around the table ended at Betsy. "Why can't you help me? Why are you frozen in time, too? You're my helper, you need to help me!"

She knew she sounded frantic, eyes moist with unshed tears, but she didn't know what she was doing.

Viera swung her hands out in desperation. "I need help!"

Gandalf's walking stick appeared in her right hand. Her jaw dropped open. "What the fuck are you doing here? Are you going to help me? Do you have some sort of solution?"

The stick pulsated in her hand.

She snarled. "That isn't an answer."

Knowing she was being unreasonable, she clutched the walking stick and shut her eyes. She had to figure this out. *Why can't I reverse time if I can stop it?*

Her mind slowly stopped spiraling, the pounding in her chest slowed, and it almost felt like a cool breeze ruffled her short hair. Viera finally took a slow, deep, breath. Like walking a path in the woods, her mind found a rhythm, and slowly, the patterns appeared. The walking stick warmed.

When she was young, her grandmother taught her to knit. She wasn't good, and she only had the patience for small things, like hats or scarves. Sometimes, in the middle of a row, something wouldn't look right; her grandmother told her to pull the yarn, undo the stitches, and respool the yarn in the skein.

Viera imagined doing that with the conversation and coffee. She only needed to pull a few stitches—moments—until the coffee was all back in the mug. Her mind replayed the coffee mug being hit, and Scout's dramatic reaction. Once she knew what she wanted, Viera released her magic and nearly fell to the floor.

The cacophony of sound hit her, then arms grabbed her, leading her to the table. "You need to eat. After that, we need to visit Flower Prancer to discuss what just happened." Betsy sounded concerned.

"Ms. Kor, how did you get all the way over there?" Scout looked and sounded dumbfounded. "And what are you holding?"

Viera searched out Tiffany, and her mug of coffee. It was where she'd placed it originally, standing proud, unharmed by Scout. She searched Tiffany's face, but there was no red burn, no hint of being splashed with the scalding hot drink. No indication of the incident.

With trembling hands, she picked up her mug and clutched it in both hands. "Scout, will you get me another mug of coffee? I really need it this morning." She finished what was in her mug in a single gulp.

From across the table, Juniper's eyes narrowed. "Get her more food, too. I think she'll need the calories." Juniper turned to Betsy. "Magic takes extra food, right?"

Betsy smiled at the other woman. "Exactly so."

Viera started eating her first breakfast. She was feeling more and more like a hobbit. First breakfast, then she'd have second. *Maybe third would be on the schedule.* "Betsy, if I'm visiting Flower Prancer, should I have another soak first?"

Her friend smiled a bit evilly. "Probably not a bad idea."

## If I Could Turn Back Time

### Viera

The trip to Torville Station Number Six wasn't long. Viera had hoped she could avoid the training rooms, and Flower Prancer in general, for the few days it took to fly to the space station. She figured once they got there she could avoid the yonat because he'd be busy, and she'd be way beneath his notice.

She sat in the training room with Betsy. The pencil on the table was still the only decoration. The wall that could become a mirror was back to being just a wall. "Did you know the wall could become a mirror?" Viera asked her friend.

Betsy considered it. "I didn't. I've never been down here, but it doesn't surprise me. It's a training room. These rooms are usually pretty flexible. They can meet the needs of trainers and trainees. That wall is probably a supersized panel ready to do anyone's bidding."

Viera deflated. "Last time I was here, Flower Prancer sent me off to get coffee and water. He was just getting rid of me for a bit, wasn't he? That panel could've created anything he needed."

A soft chuckle was her only answer.

The door opened, and the yonat himself walked in. It amused Viera how much Flower Prancer looked like a kid's dream of a unicorn: pure white with a sparkling golden horn. His hair was a perfect rainbow, and when he wasn't gazing at her in pure disapproval, his violet eyes could be considered pretty.

His tail swished and his ire preceded him into the room. Viera could sense emotions. Kids' emotions were simple and pure, and easy to ignore. Betsy, and the other Pillars, knew how to block what they felt. Betsy had taught her skill to Thorn.

Flower Prancer, for all his arrogant Elder knowledge, either didn't know how, or didn't care. His emotions filled a space as if he stood on a hill, heralding his feelings for all to hear.

From the day the krottel had attacked Viera and opened up her magic, Flower Prancer had insisted on being her trainer. Despite his insistence, he acted as if it were a hardship. There were five wizards on Earth who were more than happy to help Viera learn, but he wouldn't hear any of it. It was like he felt guilty that she'd been kidnapped while on a station during a summit being hosted by the Elders, and his penance was teaching her.

His magical specialties didn't all match up with hers. He didn't have sensing, even though that was one of the most common non-elemental magic types. Despite being common throughout the galaxy, Zuza was the only other Earthing who had it. He'd taken to helping her learn to harness the wild third specialty the krottel had bequeathed her. Though Viera had sensing as a magic proficiency, after discussing it with Flower Prancer and the other Pillars, they'd figured it came from the krottel when they'd pushed magic into her. It wasn't naturally hers, which is why her sensing magic was so hard to control. Zuzu was doing a great job helping her to learn.

Viera's natural proficiencies were energy and time, both magic types that Flower Prancer shared. Time was almost unheard of as a non-elemental magic, so rare that Viera should be grateful for having the moody yonat as a teacher. The only type less common was imbuement, and most believed that only the dwarves had that, and there were very few of them still around.

Everyone could learn a bit of any of the specialties, but a true master had to have it naturally.

"So, Earthling, how did you mess things up today?" His tone relayed the unspoken thought that she messed something up every day.

Betsy, who'd been leaning against the wall, right leg bent with her foot up, pushed out, her anger breaking through her barrier of emotional void.

Viera held out a hand in Betsy's direction but spoke to the yonat. "I stopped and reversed time at breakfast."

Flower Prancer paused and narrowed his darkening violet eyes at her. "You did this without aid, or do you have that pocket watch of yours?"

His eyes widened. "What in blazes are you holding, Ms. Kor?"

She squeezed the walking stick and refused to wilt under his harsh criticism. "It's a walking stick, Flower Prancer."

"It glows with magic. It is more than just a stick. Tell me, were you holding that thing when you did this feat of magic? I want the full story." His disapproving glare slid to Betsy. "And what are you doing here, Pillar Doeth?"

Betsy smirked. "Well, you're the master trainer. I'm here to take notes, obviously." The dry humor that Betsy was known for probably flew right over Flower Prancer's head.

He snorted and shook his head in a horse-like motion, then returned his regard to Viera.

She nodded. Patting down her pockets, Viera felt the circular impression of the pocket watch. She hadn't even thought about slipping the artifact into her pocket that morning, it was as much a habit as her phone. Ever since she'd found it in Ghana, the watch hadn't left her person. It helped focus her magic. *Huh, I have two imbued items to help me. I wonder how unusual that is.*

She licked her lower lip, realizing it gave away her nerves. "Yes, I have the artifact in my pocket. I always do. This," she wiggled the walking stick, "was Gandalf's. It's ..." She sighed, uncertain how to explain. "The thing likes me."

"What do you mean it 'likes' you?" Flower Prancer's voice was low and gravely.

"Well, Betsy keeps locking it up in her house, and it keeps following me. I didn't bring it on the ship ... yet, here it is." Viera smiled and shrugged.

"'Likes' you." His voice and emotions were filled with disappointment.

With a huff, Viera pursed her mouth tight. Then she said, "Can we focus on my reversing time? We can spend time on this," she shook the stick again, "later."

Flower Prancer snuffled and swished his tail, obviously not willing to move on. His anger sparked from his eyes. He opened his mouth to snap at her. Viera clenched her jaw. *Why is he so fucking cantankerous all the time? Why are you mad at me? Can't we just move past this?* Viera breathed out slowly, trying to calm herself.

"Whereas I don't like you dictating our time, Ms. Kor, in this, I agree. We need to make sure you understand how to control your powers." Once Flower Prancer realized she wasn't going to respond, he shifted his focus to Betsy. "Pillar Doeth, please secure a ball. We need to focus on the time issue first."

Betsy went to the wall. "One blue bouncy ball, ten inches wide."

The ball appeared and Betsy bounced it to test if it were what she wanted. Satisfied, she turned to Flower Prancer. "What now, Elder?"

He faced Viera. "Pillar Doeth will toss the ball to you. You will freeze it in time. If you can do that, I want you to reverse time to move it back to her. That is our goal for today. I do not expect success; that would be unheard of." He said that last bit quietly, as if only to himself. "So don't feel bad when you fail."

*With such motivation, no wonder I'm thriving as his student. Asshole.*

Viera smiled and faced Betsy, who rolled her eyes. She tossed the ball and Viera barely had time to catch the ball, much less figure out how to stop time.

She threw the ball back, then leaned the walking stick against the wall. As she did, she thought about what she'd felt in the dining room. *Don't fail, Viera, just don't fail.*

Betsy tossed the ball again and Viera lifted her hands thinking 'stop.' The ball didn't stop, but since her hands were up, she snatched the ball from the air.

It took five tosses for her to stop the ball. The problem was everything in the room stopped—everything except Flower Prancer. He sniffed in disapproval. "Well, at least you can stop time, that's a start. You just need to learn control, Ms. Kor."

She turned to him. "Could you stop a single item the first time you tried?"

"This isn't about me, Ms. Kor, this is about you. It's your lesson. I'm getting tired of this room and having to repeat myself as if you're a toddler. Now, take the ball. You can practice on your own by throwing the ball against the wall. If you take a ven or two into the room with you, you'll know if you've stopped only the ball."

She was surprised at the helpfulness of his suggestion but annoyed at his belittling her. His evasion of her question, however, didn't surprise her.

It didn't take her long to start time back up and catch the ball. Flower Prancer had left, so she explained to Betsy the outcome of the lesson.

They decided to have lunch and then Viera wanted to spend time relaxing and studying. She knocked on Scout's door. "Hi, kiddo. I'm planning on trying out the new app Juniper made for me. I'm going to study in your mom's room. I think I want ven therapy. Can I take Fezzik with me?"

"Sure, but Mom may not be happy when she sees that. You know her opinion of the ven."

Viera gave him a conspiratorial grin. "I'll take my chances."

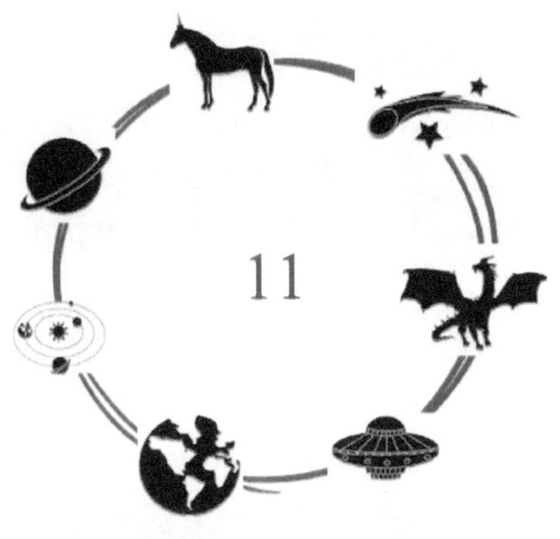

## Clash Of The Titans

### Thorn

Exhausted, Thorn trudged to her room. She wanted to go knock on Viera's door and drag her to her bed to cuddle, but she didn't have that kind of energy.

When she arrived at her room, she found Viera curled in her bed. The sight would've warmed her to her core, if it weren't for the tawny baby ven, Fezzik, curled up on her hip, small snores coming from both of them. The ven's black antenna bobbed as he breathed.

Thorn wanted to kick the small creature from her bed. Scout knew the ven weren't allowed in here, but Viera didn't. She loved that she could slide into bed and wrap her arms around the other woman. Was it worth allowing the one pet, that Viera obviously loved, to make the woman happy?

*How hard have I fallen for this Earthling? Gah! In a year or two, I'm going to head home, and what will happen then?* She shook her head. *Don't leave the Pedesterizer before you put on the breaks and enjoy the moment.*

With a grunt, Thorn stripped off her uniform, found a clean silk tank top, and tucked herself in behind Viera. The other woman shimmied closer, like the moth Fezzik resembled to a flame, until her body molded to Thorn. Releasing a content sigh, Thorn wrapped her arm around her bedmate, and gave her a small squeeze. It felt like something within her settled from the rightness of the moment. Not even the inclusion of the ven could ruin it

Thorn wrapped her body around Viera's, the big spoon to Viera's small. Fezzik stretched, placing a small paw on her hip. Ignoring that, Thorn shut her eyes and imagined what life would be like with this Earthling—her Earthling—living with her on Abritos. She knew she told herself nothing but fantasy stories, but she was winding down for sleep, and envisioning this future gave her happy dreams.

Thorn woke up to a lithe body moving along hers, hands wrapped in her hair. A warm mouth pressed against hers and an enticing tongue traced her lips, as if asking for entrance. With a low moan, she pulled Viera atop her and opened her mouth, deepening the kiss.

Viera rotated her hips, gyrating above, breath rough with her excitement.

Not wanting this lovely dream to end, Thorn kept her eyes shut as her right hand lazily drew circles and designs down Viera's silky back. When she got to Viera's panties, she traced the waist band, reveling in the other woman's tremors and groans. The more she played, the tighter Viera's hand got in her hair.

Thorn slid her hands under the elastic band to Viera's most intimate areas. She let herself stroke and rub gently, loving the sounds the other women made. Gasping, Viera pushed Thorn back. "I want more."

"Mmm, you do? Like what?" Thorn wasn't sure if she should be amused or offended. She finally opened her eyes to see the vision of bed-headed beauty above her.

Viera shut her eyes, as if embarrassed, or bracing herself for what she'd say next. "I want to taste you as you scream out your orgasm."

*Ah, amused then. I can work with this.*

"Well, my Earthing lover, if you must know, I want the same thing." Thorn raised a single eyebrow. "What if you straddle me backwards and we both get what we want?"

Viera leaned down to kiss Thorn hard and deeply in answer.

After thoroughly exploring her mouth, Viera slid off the panties, and moved to the position Thorn suggested. As Thorn pulled Viera's hips down to lick the sex hovering above her, already glistening with her excitement, Viera began her own tongue investigation.

Thorn rotated her hips up to give better access, her own heat building. She slowly dragged Viera's clit between her teeth as she pushed two fingers deep into the other woman, plunging, in and out, in and out, deep and rhythmic.

Lost in the sensations Viera created within her, and the licking and teasing she returned, she almost missed as the muscles in Viera's body began to tighten. As Thorn sucked on Viera's clit, the other woman screamed out. She'd been close enough that Viera's orgasmic yells and pleasure spasms were enough to put her over.

The joy of the moment washed through her. Wave after wave of the heat that had been building up crashed as she quivered and groaned out her own release.

Again, she marveled at how well the two of them matched. Though not from the same world, they worked each other's bodies well.

Viera turned and cuddled into her. "Morning, sunshine."

"Mmm, morning, my fire cloud." Thorn purred low. "I didn't expect to wake up like that."

Viera's arm slid around her waist and a leg entwined with hers. "I didn't want you to be late for work, and I wasn't sure you had an alarm set."

A laugh burst out of Thorn. "That's your solution for an alarm clock?"

A content hum escaped Viera as she relaxed further into Thorn. "No, that was you. I was just going to give you a morning kiss."

The ven landed on Viera's shoulder, turned, then walked down to her hip. He turned again then settled. Thorn let out a gusty sigh. "Fezzik ... in my space?"

"Scout did warn me. I meant to return him, but he's so soft and cuddly." She looked at the creature. I'll bring him back on my way to my room. We arrive at Torville Station Number Six today, right? I should pack and get ready."

Thorn's head fell back on her pillow, her responsibilities slamming back to mind. "Yeah, and on that note, my lovely lady, I should shower and head up to the bridge. I have responsibilities ... things to do today. We'll be going through the GPS within the hour, just so you know."

The lift to the bridge gave Thorn a few minutes to shift her thoughts from the naked woman in her room to the priorities of the day. *Not enough time.* She'd stopped by the dining hall for a breakfast sandwich and mug of coffee, then grabbed a second mug before heading up to command. She needed to be sharp if they were meeting with members of the many alien races today.

The door slid open, and she stepped out, ready to lead. "Report. Where is the krottel ship? Is it still headed towards Earth? Is it enough to warn them? Are there any near the GPS? How long until we enter? Are there any friendlies around?"

Horax's blue scales shimmered in the bright bridge lights. "The krottel ship turned away from Earth, as if that wasn't their destination. Then it stopped. We aren't sure what their deal is; they've ignored all communication from us, from the Earth, and from the Elders. No other ships around the GPS, krottel or friendly. We'll be entering in twenty-three minutes, Commander Firoza."

A tension settled over her as she headed to her seat. As her nerves played within her, she felt stronger and ready to face the space station as a leader of her people.

Before the krottel came to Abritos, Thorn had been a baker. She'd been hired by the capital city, a six-hour glide from her home, but she transported like all of her people did, to cater a Tamberin, a celebration of the coming of snow and the cold season.

When the krottel came, several of the key leaders died in the first waves of the attack. Thorn stepped up, not wanting her people to succumb to the bugs. Desperate for leadership, the chanzii listened to her, heard what she said, and realized she brought wisdom to the table.

She'd only gone home to collect Scout and Beaver. She'd never returned to her bakery.

At times, she worried the people she led would see her as a fraud, but over the years she'd done too much, been too strong, and now she knew she was the Commander they titled her. When she landed on Earth, part of her wanted to try baking again, but all of the ingredients were wrong, and the chemistry was different. She could've downloaded recipes and learned, but she had another job to focus on, and she didn't want to reinvent her old life on Earth. It was too painful.

Now that the prospect of returning home loomed closer and closer, recipes danced in her head.

Horax's low gravelly voice reverberated through the bridge. "Five minutes to GPS."

"Contact the portal and begin the launching steps. I'd like to get to the other side of the galaxy as soon as possible. I know Tiffany and her parents would like that, too."

Her crew grumbled and she smirked.

*I wonder how many of them have heard about the hunger strike. As long as none of us mention it, we can pretend it's not happening. I'm not even sure what they expect. We can't find sea water in the void of space! Gah! It's their choice, and we'll be docking at Torville Station Number Six by the end of the day. Silly creatures.*

Horax's voice pulled her back to the bridge. "Approaching the GPS."

A wavering in the stars ahead signaled that the ancient device was activated. "Forward ahead, keep it steady, and get us to that space station."

"Acknowledged, Commander Firoza."

Though some said going through the portal didn't feel like anything, Thorn felt a tightening of the air around her, then a pulling, as if she was being squeezed out of a tight space. It only lasted a few moments. Once the air released her, she huffed out a breath and slumped. "Take us to Torville Station Number Six, helm."

"Still no signs of the krottel, Commander Firoza. It looks like they've cleared out of this sector. We've contacted the other chanzii ships in the area, and none of them have picked up any of their ships."

During the trip to the station, they periodically scanned the skies for the krottel. They knew there was a chance they'd run into the bugs while at the space station, but so far everything was clear.

"Thank you, Horax. Ask Juniper to set up a monitoring schedule. I'd like to be informed if any of them pop up while we're here. She should coordinate with all of our ships."

"Will do, ma'am."

The rest of the tip was uneventful, and soon they docked in the port the station lieutenant assigned them. Thorn checked the station's time: G-twenty. By the time everyone found their assigned rooms, it would be time for dinner and rest. Adjusting to the thirty-hour rotation would be jarring for the shortness of their stay. Beyond dropping Tiffany and her parents off, there wasn't a ton more they had to do. Just a meeting with the other leaders of her planet.

*Maybe visit Abritos.* Her heart hurt at the thought of going home. It had been so long. She missed the rolling countryside, the recognizable trees and flowers, and the clean smell of the land. Moreover, she feared what the bugs may have done to change the landscape she and her people loved.

"I'm going to go find Scout and get him herded with the ven to our room. The ship should be fine in the hands of a skeleton crew."

There was a round of agreements as she headed to the lift.

She found Scout in his room, packing. "Good, you're here. We're going to disembark now." The chaos of the ven seemed somehow ... less. "Where are ..." she squinted. "Westley, the miscreant, and Buttercup, the one-and-only well-behaved?"

Her son's face blossomed into a large smile. "They're old enough to not need Beaver and Betsy wanted them. I thought while we're here, we're all living close enough it would be a great test run."

One of Thorn's eyebrows rose. "She ... wanted them. Like both of them? A matched set?"

Scout began to bounce. "Yes! She's been eyeing them since Beaver had them. She loves the ven. Just because you think they're obnoxious doesn't mean others don't see the wonderfulness of them."

Thorn shook her head. "Whatever. How soon until you're ready to go?"

"Um, maybe ten minutes?"

"Perfect, me too. I'm going to check on Viera and then we can be off."

She tapped in the code to alert Viera. The door swung open and there Viera stood, eyes bright, with a huge smile. "I was thrown from the bed ... again. The docking always seems to throw me, literally. But are we heading on to the station now?"

Her words tumbled out of her, as fast as her apparent fall from her bed. "I need to finish packing. You're good?"

Viera nodded. "I am. I didn't unpack. I figured we wouldn't be long on the ship. I'm ready to explore other alien races with more of an open mind this time."

"Good. I'll be back in a few minutes. Take one more look to make sure you have everything, and we'll be off."

The halls were crowded once they exited the Ziner. Most of the crew didn't want to pack and relocate to Torville Station Number Six for only a few days. Tiffany and her parents were the first to exit, barely saying good-bye in their haste to leave the ship behind.

As they had last time, Viera shared a family suite with Scout and Thorn. The apartments had enough rooms for all of them, though Thorn dragged the Earthling into her room. She wasn't going to waste any more time apart. She wasn't sure how long she had before her people started moving home. *Demanding the return, really. Not that I can blame them.*

Once their bags were dropped off, they headed to the main promenade for dinner.

Flower Prancer was there. He approached, sliding amongst all the creatures crowding the open-air market and food stands. Then a new creature sauntered up to them, a dwarf. Thorn blinked; she hadn't expected to see a dwarf. They were rarely seen off their planet. This one was the only one who seemed to come out from hiding, and Thorn knew him. "Viera, I'd like you to meet Balzeno. Balzeno, Viera."

The wide man-looking creature with an auburn beard reaching his knees and thick hair pinned back in leather string and braids, bowed low before turning his bright green eyes to her. His deep bass voice reverberated, and Thorn felt like she could feel it to her toes. "Ah! The new Pillar to Earth, the talk of the galaxy. I had hoped you'd return to be met by one as lowly as me."

Viera's eyes widened as he spoke. She inclined her head in a small bow. "Sir dwarf, the honor is all mine. It brings me nothing but pleasure to meet you."

The words tickled Thorn. It was good to give respect to the Elders, especially the dwarves.

Flower Prancer arrived. "Balzeno, you escaped the confines of your planet. I did not know that was possible."

Balzeno's face hardened. "Just because my people enjoy my company, unlike some Elders I could mention, does not make my spending time on-planet odd. You should try not being so abrasive, youngling."

Flower Prancer snuffled, then turned to Thorn. "I'll find us a table. We should discuss tomorrow's meeting." With a swish of his tail, he left.

Once the yonat departed, Balzeno's face broke into a smile. "I have a duty right now, Pillar Viera of Earth, but I'd love to have time to learn more about you. But until that time, I have some advice. The magic within you is yours. There is a pattern in our proficiencies, but it behaves within the limits of our being. In the end, it's yours, not your trainer's." He winked as he walked off.

Eyes wide, Viera turned to Thorn. "What did he mean?"

Thorn shrugged. "I'm not sure. I guess it's something about your lessons."

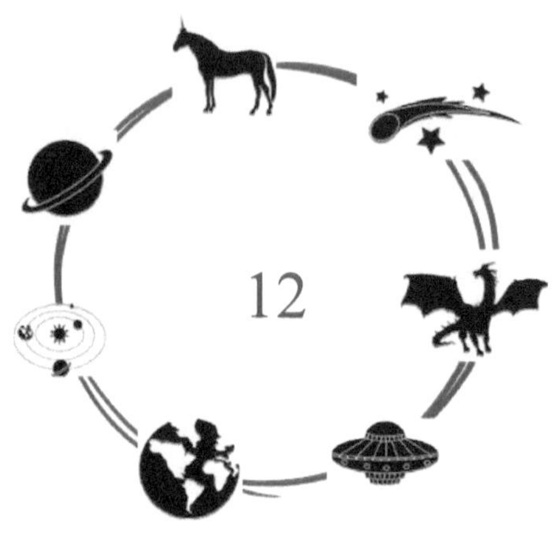

## Wait, What Did I Miss?

### Viera

Viera stretched, trying not to dislodge the weight resting on her hip. Opening her eyes, she gazed down the length of her body. Tawny like his mother, Fezzik curled on her, asleep, his long black antenna vibrating with his snores.

"Morning, sleepyhead. Where are your brothers and sisters? And how did you get in here? I thought Thorn didn't allow you into the room."

Thorn's voice came from the bathroom. "I let him in once I was dressed. I need to get to my meeting. I'll see you later." She came through the ensuite door and smirked. "And you're calling the pet lazy? You're still lollygagging about, Ms. Kor." She came over to give Viera a gentle kiss. "I would love to have the time to just be with you. We're both way too busy."

"Hmm." Viera shifted position and looked up at Thorn. Fezzik rolled to Thorn's side of the bed and went back to sleep. "I agree. Let's run away and spend a week together ignoring our responsibilities."

Thorn laughed. "Sounds perfect."

Once she left, Viera got up and headed to the shower. She had to wash and then soak in magic. *I don't know what's in store for me, but if Flower Prancer doesn't have a lesson planned, I still need to master bouncing a ball and having it move back in time. Gah! Why isn't any of this easy? Magic is so cool, but the damn unicorn acts like it should all be intuitive, which it's not.*

Dressed, Viera made her way to the main room to find food. She knew that soon, the thirty-hour clock of the space station would start to mess with her, but for now, her watch told her it was seven in the morning, she'd just woken up, and she needed coffee.

Outside the room she shared with Thorn there was a kitchen/dining room combination and a living room. A door led to Scout's room, and down a hall was a third. Last time she came to the station she'd stayed in that room.

Sitting at the small round table in the kitchen, Scout drank from a dark mug. "Aren't you a bit young to be drinking coffee?" She knew chronologically the boy was close to her age, but by his species standards, he was the equivalent to an eight-year-old.

His face broke into a huge smile as three baby ven flew at Viera, landing on her shoulders and head. This made Scout laugh, almost tumbling from his chair. Once he caught his breath, his eyes continued to shine. "It's juice. Do you want coffee here, or should we head to the promenade for breakfast? I'm guessing we can find Tiffany." His brow scrunched. "Oh, and Betsy and maybe Horax, if he's not already training."

Viera debated if she was ready to face a gaggle of aliens before she'd had liquid reinforcement.

After a moment of consideration, and a few stabs of ven talons in her skin, she sighed. "Yeah, let's go. If Tiffany is leaving today, I'd like to say goodbye. I'm going to miss her."

"Me, too." Scout's demeanor changed as his shoulders drooped, and his face fell. "I don't know why her parents won't let her continue to live on Earth, just for a bit longer. It's all she's known. She's going to be scared without friends on her home planet."

Walking over to stand next to Scout, Viera squatted down. "She needs to meet friends of her own species." She ruffled his hair. "I know you're going to miss her—we all are—but this really is the best thing for her."

His face scrunched up. "Okay, fine, but let's find her now and ask if she wants to have breakfast with us. She said she'd watch Horax's training with me today."

"Okay, let's go. But first," Viera reached up to scratch her riders, "have these three eaten?"

"Yeah, Mom told me to make sure I took care of them. Once we leave, they'll calm down. They just miss Beaver, who's off socializing." Scout got up to help remove the ven from Viera before she stood up.

There weren't many beings in the hallways this early in the morning, so Viera was shocked to discover the promenade filled with them. She stopped and took a second to let the sounds wash over her. The sight of so many different types of aliens of different sizes, colors, and types froze her in her tracks for a moment.

A scream cut through the sounds of the room. She knew the voice, she knew the scream, she knew the person. *Tiffany is in trouble.*

Heart pounding, hands trembling, mind focused on helping her former student, Viera ran. When she found the small girl, she squatted down, using Gandalf's staff for balance, and put a hand on the young lady's shoulder. She followed Tiffany's gaze up and saw a flock of phoenixes flying out of a tunnel leading from the roof. Their feathers were red and orange with highlights of yellow—they looked like flying fire.

Under Viera's hand, her former student shook.

The last time Viera came to Torville Station Number Six, she didn't notice there were hallways up above for the flying aliens, but as she watched the movement near the ceiling, she realized it made perfect sense.

"Tiffany, they're phoenixes. You're fine, sweetie."

Tiffany breathed in shakily. "Ms. Kor, where did you come from?" With an effort, moving her face before her eyes, she stared at Viera. "I'm not scared, just startled. They looked like fireballs flying at me. But look at them, they're mesmerizing."

Gazing back up at the flying beauties, Viera watched as they perched on some of the areas built for them, socializing with a group of griffins and ven.

Shaking her head, Viera rubbed Tiffany's back. "I ran up from the lift when I heard you yelp, dear. You were just focused on the phoenixes and didn't see me approach."

Huffing and puffing, Scout pounded up, his feet echoing on the floor. It occurred to Viera that it was odd she could hear his steps in the room that had been so loud moments before. Her body tense, Viera pushed up and gazed around her.

"Ms. Kor, that was amazing. I didn't know you could teleport!" Scout's voice reverberated through the now silent room.

His words hit her like a bucket of ice water. "What?" Turning again, she realized all the beings in the room were emanating shock and awe. Her hands trembled. "I ... but I didn't. I ran. I remember my feet hitting the floor, navigating around the others on my way over here." Her heart pounded faster as she dropped her gaze to Scout. "You didn't see me run?"

Scout's face scrunched up. "You just disappeared, and then when I got here, you were here." His brow furrowed more, and his head tilted. "With that walking stick. Did you have that before?"

Viera gaped at her hand. It suddenly occurred to her that she hadn't had it before. *For fuck's sake, walking stick, why did you appear? Why do I need you? How did I get here so fast?*

Her body began to feel numb as the questions whirled in her mind. Tiffany and her parents joined in the mass of alien eyes boring into her, demanding answers. The problem was, she didn't have any answers to give.

*Where is Betsy? I'd even take Flower Prancer at this point.*

A commotion to her left had her whipping around. Pushing past a large dark orange qynad, the size of a moving-truck, and a fing, Balzeno stomped out into the open area towards Viera. When he got close, his beard stretched in what Viera assumed was a smile. "Youngling, what mischief are you causing so early in the morning?"

She sighed. "I have no idea. I heard a yelp and ran, but no one saw it. They say I just appeared. I don't know what happened. I feel like I never know what's happening." She knew by the end she sounded pitiful.

The dwarf's eyes narrowed. "You need more training."

She grunted. "Training is all I do."

He chuckled. "You've only been in this world a short time, young wizard. Don't be hasty. Frustration in the path won't make you learn faster, it will only make the journey less pleasurable."

The advice, though different from how she would've worded it, felt like a lesson she could've given her students. "Thank you. You're right. I need to spend more time practicing. I wish there was a book explaining all of the different nuances and how everything combines."

He nodded. "There are some common threads, but the magic is yours and how you mix what's yours is always going to be a bit different than the next wizard."

The words settled in her. "So, I need to practice."

"Yes." His low-pitched voice echoed through the room. As they spoke, the others went back to what they'd been doing, as if realizing there really was nothing to see.

"But there seems to be so much to learn. Every few days there's something new."

He reached out and rubbed her arm. "And that's the best part. The adventure of something new around every turn. It will take time to figure it all out and even longer to master any of it. But the path should be fun."

She smiled, remembering all the times she'd mocked books and movies where the people who had to do magic homework whined, and she rolled her eyes. She'd been jealous. Now here she was, in the same situation. "Thank you, Balzeno."

She meant it. He'd given her a clarity she'd been missing since all of this began.

Shifting his gaze, he let his eyes travel up and down Gandalf's walking stick. "Well, hello old friend." He traced his finger down the side. "This silly piece of wood will help you, if you keep it with you. It's a fine piece of magic, for something created by an Earthling." The last was said with a heavy amount of derision. "The more you keep it around you, the stronger your bond will be. It's why you found your speed so early in your magic."

"My ... speed?"

"Yes, youngling. You don't think you actually teleported, do you? With a proficiency in time, an unusual skill, you have a huge array of possibilities. Add in there a bit of the energy proficiency, and you get speed. From what I've learned from some of the other Elders, when the krottel opened up your magic, they pushed their sensing ability into you, which is why it's so wild. Naturally having time and energy is so incredibly rare, dear, that I'm looking forward to seeing the trouble you'll get into."

A sense of dread hit her. "Trouble?"

"Oh, yes. A new wizard who's already an Elder? You're going to keep me young." With a wink and a nod, he moved away.

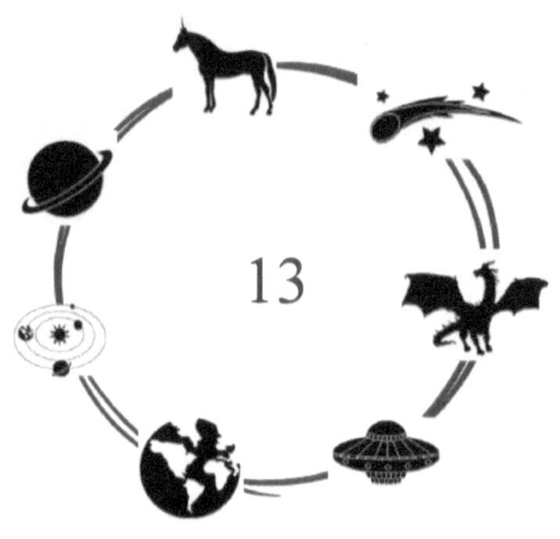

## 13

## Time To Get Back To Work

### Viera

Viera sat at the table with Scout, Tiffany, and Tiffany's parents. She finally had a mug of coffee, and hugged it to herself, trying to recover from the shock of the last few minutes. She needed to write down all the skills she'd picked up and set up her own training schedule. She'd been practicing with Betsy and Flower Prancer, but she was a big girl, not a kid in school. When she dug deep within herself, she realized that this was not only something she needed to master; it was something she wanted to do.

"But I'm scared." Tiffany's voice was low.

Shaking herself from her ruminations, Viera turned to the kids. Scout's head tilted. "Why are you scared?"

Tiffany's mom tutted. "If Tiffany doesn't want to go, then don't try to force her. Let my daughter make her own decisions. You aren't her boss or a tour guide."

Every time Viera was around these two, she had to work at not rolling her eyes or snapping at them. Despite having lived on Earth for years, they didn't seem to know how to interact with other beings. She took a slow, steadying breath. "He's not trying to force Tiffany to do anything she doesn't want to do, he just wanted to learn what made her say 'no.'" A quick glance at the kids showed they were both relaxed. "On the ride here they were both excited to watch Horax train."

Tiffany's dad's face hardened. "You mean on one of those days you kept our daughter away from us?"

Betsy walked up to the table, grabbing a chair from a nearby table and adding it to theirs. "I don't know that keeping a kid in a single room is fair, but," she put her hands up as she sat, "I know that Tiffany's upbringing isn't my concern. That said, where she goes and what she does is also not up to Viera. She and Scout played games and learned Galactic Standard; something Tiffany needs to learn. I don't know exactly what you're angry about."

Though Betsy sounded cordial, there was steel behind her words that Viera could feel. Apparently, she, too, was tired of Tiffany's parents' antics.

"Don't judge us, wizard."

Betsy gazed blankly at them for a moment, then turned to Viera. "I hear you made a splash this morning, friend."

Viera sighed, taking a sip of her coffee. "I'm going to finish my breakfast then go practice."

Scout groaned. "Not you, too! Who's going to watch Horax with me?"

Betsy reached across the table and patted his hands. "I'll head down to the training fields with you. It's been awhile, and I hear Horax is doing great this year."

Scout's face transformed, a smile taking over the pout he'd been sporting. "Yes!"

Tiffany sat stiff in her seat, shoulders hunched, eyes wide. She slowly turned her head towards her parents. "Mom, Dad, would it be okay if I went with Scout and Ms. Doeth to watch Horax?" For a moment Viera thought she'd say more, but then she bit her lip and trembled slightly, as if scared of what her parents might say or do.

Upper lip twitching, Kelpweaver, Tiffany's mom, glared first at Viera and then at Betsy. "If that's what you really want, dear, but make sure you feel safe. Return to the rooms *as soon* as it becomes too much."

Viera's body tensed. *As soon, not if. Her mom passed judgment without letting Tiffany enjoy the experience.*

Betsy placed a hand on Viera's arm but gazed back at Tiffany's mom. "Be assured, Kelpweaver, if Tiffany wants to return to your rooms, I'll personally escort her. She'll never be alone."

After the meal, Viera headed back to the rooms she shared with Thorn and Scout. As fun as it was to watch the training fields, she knew she had to practice her own magic. If she were younger, the slow mastery of her art would be fine, but she had adult responsibilities. She'd just become one of the Pillars of Earth, and there were only six. With so few, she needed to know how to harness the power coursing through her body before the different proficiencies played havoc on their own.

In the suite, she went to her bags and found the blue ball from her lessons on the ship. Her first goal of the morning was to be able to stop and reverse time. She felt like she was some sort of kraken with tentacles of magic waving out of her. If she didn't start to control them, she feared the consequences. Weird pockets of time doing their own things around her, while sensing overwhelmed her.

Mostly, she knew that couldn't happen, but on some level it was a fear. She'd seen movies with bubbles of time popping all around the main character and she really didn't want that happening to her.

Not wanting to run into other people, she decided to practice in the guest room the suite provided. She walked towards the empty room. When she opened the door, Fezzik darted in, flying above her. With a sigh, she shook her head and decided not to fight the young ven. She didn't want a hoard of flying creatures, so shut the door before any more of the rascals could fly or dash in.

Viera sat on the bed and the ven perched on her shoulder. *Well, at least he isn't on my head this time.*

Her plan was to throw the ball against the wall and as it flew back, stop it and reverse time until it touched the wall again. Hopefully she could isolate her power to just the ball and not everything in the room.

With a calming breath, Viera focused deep within herself to find her central well of magic. Once she felt she'd found it, she tossed the ball at the wall opposite her. After it bounced, she bent the time around the ball to make the ball stop. To her surprise, it did. The rock on her shoulder told her the ven sat frozen as well.

"Fuck." Both her hands faced the ball. She flicked her hands outward and released her spell. The ball flew towards her, and she caught it.

On her shoulder, the ven wiggled. "I know, my friend, not quite what we wanted. We'll have to try something else." She reached up to scratch the soft moth-like creature, who immediately began to make purring sounds of contentment.

Viera shut her eyes, imagining what she wanted: the time around the ball to stop so that she could reverse it, meanwhile the time around the rest of the room to remain in motion. After one more meditative breath she raised her arm. Fezzik, his annoyance at all her motions seeping into her mind like a buzz of white noise, leapt to the air and hovered above her. She shot a glance at him before lifting her arm to toss the ball.

Fezzik dipped and flew in a circle as the ball flew, hit the wall, and bounced. His butt wagged in anticipation. Hands out towards the ball, Viera released some of her magic, and ... everything froze. She gazed at the ball and the ven both frozen in the air and sighed. With a frustrated wave of her hands, she released the magic and caught the ball, thinking back on everything that had happened, wondering if there was anything she could've done differently, better.

Fezzik happily flew and chased his tail. Viera snorted, relaxing as she watched him. *I wonder what he'd do if we got him a string skirt? He'd be chasing the tassels attached to him for weeks. We'd have to make a video. I wonder if the alien world has an equivalent of a silly home video show?*

Viera shook her head and tossed the ball. As it hit the wall, she focused with both hands out, palms towards the ball. She pushed a bit of magic out as she beat both hands forward as if giving someone a high ten. As before, the ball stopped. Freezing time was becoming easier for her.

A sound above her made her body quiver with hope. Slowly staring up, she realized Fezzik still spun above her. "Fezzik! I did it. The ball is frozen and you're not."

She wanted to dance, but knew she'd only done half the drill. *I don't even know if I can repeat what I've done.*

Shaking out her hands, she dug deeper into her memory of Tiffany being burnt by her coffee. What she'd felt, her fear and her need for that moment not to happen. *I need to undo the thing.*

Trying to relax into her magic, Viera pushed out a bit of her will.

She watched, slack-jawed, as the ball flew back towards the wall, exactly how she'd hoped it would, flying back in time. *I did it! Oh, my God above, I actually did it! I can't believe I stopped the ball in time and reversed it!*

As her eyes widened in shock and pleasure, her joy morphed to horror as the ball hit the far wall, splatting with a sickly sound, looking like it melted into the wall. Viera gulped, disgusted with what she saw. "What the actual fuck did I do?"

Even the ven seemed to vibrate with questions as Viera leapt up to investigate her failure. The ball slid slowly down the wall, deformed. When Viera brought her hand close to it, she felt heat radiating from it. *Fuck, I must've doubled up my magical push. I need to get a new ball, and food. I'm feeling dizzy as well as defeated.*

Disappointed, Viera walked out to the main area and ordered up a bowl of mac and cheese and another ball—green, ten inches in diameter. Then, after some consideration, she asked for a glass of red wine.

She considered feeding the ven, but knew they were on a strict diet. Scout and Thorn knew all the details.

Once she'd eaten and finished her wine, she headed back to the room. As before, Fezzik followed her.

Fezzik flew around. Stopping the ball in time felt easier. This time, she only used one hand—two felt like overkill. She knew what she needed to do; it was a skill she felt was in her bag of tricks. Clearing her mind, she focused on moving the ball back in time without heating it up. Just before she reversed time, Fezzik dropped down to play with the ball. Both he and the ball flew in different directions, being dragged back in their own timelines.

Her heart dropped as she watched the ven, making sure the spell hadn't heated him or harmed him in any way. A small manic laugh echoed the relief she felt when he squawked and flew towards her.

His reaction made sense as the ball slammed into her head. Viera fell back on the bed, laughing. She felt both happy with her success, and glad to be done. She followed Fezzik as he chased the ball. *I think I can do a lot more of this stressful level magic if I have a ven helping me out!*

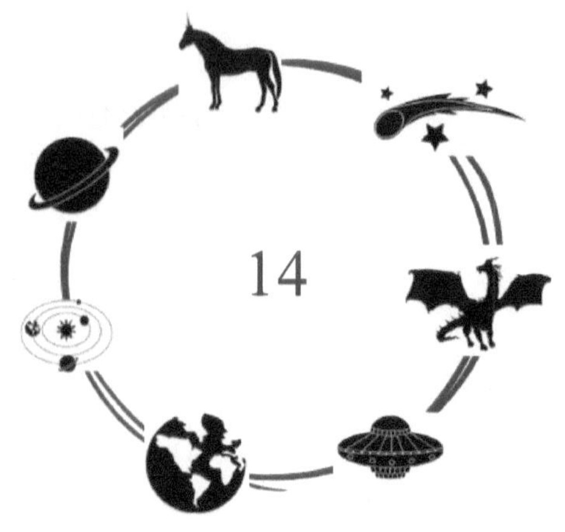

## I Need A Vacation From My Vacation!

### Thorn

"**M**ajor Shifts, please update us on Abritos." Thorn thought the Major, her leader in this quadrant, looked tired. Had he slept much since she spoke to him last?

Thorn sat at a table in a conference room in one of the lower levels of Torville Station Number Six. The previous day, she'd found Viera in the guest room asleep, a silly ven on her hip, a melted bouncy ball smeared on the wall. She wasn't sure what had happened, but she hoped the training session had ended successfully.

She knew her lover would spend time fine-tuning that time spell again today. She insisted Viera have a pile of food with her. In the conference room today, Thorn was joined by the Major, Flower Prancer, and Betsy. Yesterday, Thorn had sat and reviewed reports from all of the satellite leaders on their plans to bring the chanzii back home to Abritos. Today, she needed to figure out when their plan would be ready for fruition.

Both Flower Prancer and Betsy wanted to join in on this meeting for their own reasons. Flower Prancer because he had been the Elder representative who agreed that the Elders would stick their collective noses into other races' business. Betsy, because she was interested in staying on top of what the damn bugs were doing. The Earth Pillar was nervous about her own planet.

So far there wasn't any indication that the krottel were heading to Earth, but any information on those creatures was important.

Major Shift rubbed the back of his neck, his dark purple hair shifting over the back of his hand. "That's just the thing, Commander Firoza. Like I told you before, I don't think there are any of the krottel on Abritos. We've waited for you to get here, but we think they've already evacuated."

Flower Prancer's head snapped first to the Major and then to Thorn. "Commander Firoza? Is this true? And you haven't told me?"

She grumbled low. "Elder, I didn't have any facts. Until I knew one way or another, I didn't feel comfortable bringing anything to your attention."

His violet eyes narrowed. "And what is your plan, Commander Firoza?"

She sighed, unhappy with him dominating the meeting. "If you don't mind, Elder Flower Prancer, that *is* the point of this meeting. To discuss and decide our next move. Please give us a few minutes and you'll learn our decisions as we make them."

His tail swished with his annoyance. "Very well."

Thorn worked to not let her smirk show. "Major, how many ships do we have monitoring the planet?"

He consulted a digital pad, tapping it a few times. "We have six ships in and around the planet and its three moons. But we have more nearby, if we need them. Two have been more active in monitoring the krottel retreat."

Betsy's head tilted. "They didn't notice when the planet had emptied of the bugs or when all the krottel ships had left?"

Major Shift's hand continued to tap on the digital pad. "Well, that's the thing. There are still a few of their ships on the ground. The last ship left only a few days ago. The threshold for evacuation hasn't been met. We only checked our sensors because of the bug found on Earth."

"Ah," Betsy said, nodding. "That makes sense. But since the one bug was so hard to find, I'm assuming you need to do a closer inspection of Abritos?"

A smile took over Thorn's face as warmth bubbled up from her belly. *Home. I have an excuse to go home!* "Yes. I'll be taking a group to Abritos to check out the planet. We'll see if we can find any bugs, search the main cities they attacked, and the surrounding area. If the area is clear, we'll begin moving in groups to rebuild and then the rest can come home."

Flower Prancer snorted. "Do you really think that surveying a small area of the planet will be enough, Commander Firoza?" Contempt and disapproval dripped from his words.

Major Shift's body stiffened, and his mouth tightened. "Sir. Our sensors show the planet clear of the krottel. Our next step is rebuilding. What the Commander has planned is for us to check over the planet as we rebuild. I know you weren't implying that Commander Firoza, or any of our leaders, were negligent in their duties, Elder."

The yonat's violet eyes swung to Major Shift. "Yes, Major. I am implying that one as young as she, or you, will make silly mistakes."

Betsy snorted. "For fuck's sake, Flower Prancer, just because you're an Elder, doesn't mean you're old, do you forget that? I'm older than you, and you're barely older than these two. Major Shift is over two hundred years old."

"Two hundred and seventy-one, ma'am."

"Exactly," Betsy said, pointing at the Major. "You aren't even three hundred and fifty, Elder. So, get off your high horse and either be helpful or get out. Being judgmental of everyone is getting old ... older than you!" The Pillar of Earth glared at the yonat. *Gods, she is in no way intimidated by the Elder who scares everyone else.*

Thorn wanted to cheer.

With a swish of his tail, Flower Prancer snorted. "If you're quite done comparing our ages, Pillar Doeth, then we can move on. I do not know what horse you're talking about. I am a yonat, not a beast of burden. I am also not judgmental. Yonat only judge when asked." Thorn saw everyone in the room press their lips together, trying to hold back their reactions to his statement. "I try to help by asking the important questions. As for being helpful, I'd suggest bringing young Ms. Kor along. She may be in her infancy in her magic abilities, but her sensing is probably the best I've seen. If anyone could pick up on a krottel presence, it would be her."

Before anyone else could say anything, Thorn took control of the discussion. "That is a great idea. I was planning on taking her anyway. She doesn't know anyone else here and this gives her something to do beyond practicing language and her magic."

Next to her, Betsy nodded. "I'd like to go, as well. I haven't seen your planet in over a century." She squinted up at the ceiling. "Unless you don't want to bring Scout and need someone to stay with him. I could understand that."

Thorn wrestled with her conscience. On the one hand, she knew Scout would love to go home. He may be crushed if he weren't allowed to see Abritos. On the other hand, it wasn't safe. She licked her bottom lip as she debated her answer. "I would love to have you along. Your knowledge and magical skills would be a blessing on our travels. That said, if you could stay and help with Scout and the ven, that would be a huge weight off my shoulders."

Betsy nodded. "Then it's settled. I'm sure I can make it to your lovely land during the repopulation."

Before anything could be said, the door opened, and Juniper stuck her head in. "I'm sorry for interrupting, and for being late. Commander Firoza, did you still want me to join you in this meeting?"

Thorn smiled at her engineer. "Yes, Juniper, please come and sit down. We were just about to start talking about taking a skeleton crew to Abritos. Having you here to discuss numbers needed to ensure a safe round trip will be helpful."

They spent the next couple hours planning the trip, how many people they needed, how many ships, and what they'd do once there.

As Thorn approached the door of her suite, Horax lumbered out. The dragon smiled wide. "Commander, it's nice to see you."

She tilted her head. "Horax. Is everything okay?"

"Yes, ma'am. After winning my round and getting my free meal on the promenade, Scout had a fun project for me. You know him, always up to something."

Thorn wasn't sure if she was excited or apprehensive to hear her son was up to planning things, but she smiled. "There are new orders in your inbox for tomorrow. I'm glad you got some time with Scout before we head out."

"We're leaving?"

"Yes, but we can discuss that later. Have a good night, Horax."

"You, too, Commander."

Thorn opened the door to her unit and the spicy scent of food permeated the air. Her belly grumbled. Inside, Viera and Scout sat waiting for her in the kitchen. On the table sat a huge bowl surrounded by smaller vessels.

Viera smiled wide. "Beef curry, rice, chicken satay, and crab Rangoon. Are you as hungry as I am?"

"Gods yes! This is an amazing surprise. While we eat, we can discuss my day as well as yours."

Scout filled his plate, then took a huge bite of fried crab. "Tiffany and I went back to the training fields. Since Betsy was with you, Tiffany's dad came with us. He hated it, so we only watched Horax. Then we went to her place, and I helped her practice Galactic Standard. She's super-fast."

He spoke so quickly, his words tripped over themselves. Once done, he dug into his food. The smile on Viera's face as she watched Scout warmed Thorn's heart. She loved how much the other woman loved her son. Part of her yearned for this to be more than a short-term thing. She knew Scout loved his former teacher, too. But Viera was needed on Earth.

After finishing her own bite of curry, Viera said, "I spent most of the morning making sure I could move a ball back through time. It's only a few seconds, but I think I can do it. I'm not sure of any practical application of the magic, but it's nice to gain control of my abilities. Each time I figure something out, it's like a puzzle piece that is me is put back into place. It feels nice."

Thorn tilted her head. "So, you can move on then?"

Viera snorted a humorless laugh. "No, I'll have to keep playing with this, looking at it from different angles, so that I really understand the dynamics of it. Magic is a rich, multi-dimensional beast, and if I don't comprehend all the nuances, I could hurt someone, or myself. However, I've learned the first step. As the saying goes, you need to learn how to walk before you can run."

"Okay, that makes sense ... mostly." Thorn took a few bites of curry. The flavors exploded in her mouth. "This is fantastic. I didn't know the panel could create anything like this."

Scout bounced in his seat, practically dancing. "Ms. Kor and I spent like an hour figuring out how to program in these recipes. We had to call Horax to help us. We wanted to surprise you with something she loved." He glowed with excitement.

Viera reached over and ruffled his hair. "I thought we were going to keep that our little secret."

He blushed. "Sorry, Ms. Kor."

Thorn laughed. "It's okay. I appreciate it even more."

"What about your day?" Viera poured some wine for herself and Thorn. Then she took a sip, waiting for Thorn's reply.

"I spent most of my time looking over reports and having a meeting. We've decided that tomorrow a group of us will head to Abritos, to make sure the krottel have really left." Out of the corner of her eye, she saw Scout start to vibrate with excitement. "Sorry, kiddo, you can't come. This is a military engagement. If we find any krottel, it may not be safe. You'll be staying here with—"

He sighed. "Ms. Kor?"

Thorn gave him a small smile. Before she could answer, Viera turned to him. "It'll be great. We can continue our language lessons. You know I want to become fluent."

He perked up a bit at that.

With a sigh, Thorn continued. "Actually, Viera, you'll be coming with us. Believe it or not, that was Flower Prancer's suggestion. We need to determine if there are any bugs on the planet, and your ability to sense them is one of the best." She turned to her son. "Betsy agreed to stay with you. I believe she has some plans to make your time fun."

His face scrunched up before he nodded. "We've talked about starting to train the young ven. I bet that's what she's thinking." He seemed to perk up a bit.

As much as Thorn got annoyed at the flying beasts, if they worked to distract Scout, she'd be grateful for their presence on the trip.

"I get to see your planet?" Viera's voice was soft, but her wide eyes and slack jaw showed her shock and, Thorn hoped, excitement.

"Do you want to go?"

"Yes! I mean, absolutely. That would be amazing."

Thorn smiled, again feeling warmed by Viera's response. "It won't be a vacation—no more than any of this is a vacation."

"Not for you, maybe." Viera snorted. "But to me, I'm totally taking a secondary vacation from this vacation."

# 15

## My Tendrils Of Magic Are Explosive

### Viera

When Viera woke up, she looked at her watch, then groaned. *Gah! The hour differential between Earth and the space station really messes with my circadian rhythm. I should be having dinner right now. I feel so heavy!* She took a deep breath and pushed herself up.

After visiting the restroom, she found Thorn lying in bed watching her under lowered eyelids, a bit of a wicked smile on her face. She summoned Viera with a wave of her hand.

Viera smiled back, desire heating her. "When do we need to meet the others on the promenade?"

Thorn made an appreciative sound deep in her throat, her gaze raking up and down Viera's body. "We have time." Her voice came out low.

Swinging her hips, Viera sashayed to the bed, then climbed up onto her hands and knees. She crawled along Thorn, randomly kissing the beautiful turquoise skin: a hip, her lower belly, just below her breast. When Viera reached Thorn's face, she swooped in for a proper kiss, slow, deep, and with enough pizazz to curl Viera's toes.

Viera rubbed against Thorn, igniting sparks throughout her body. She rolled her hips, stimulating both her and Thorn's sex.

While she moved, Thorn's hands reached up, stroking her chest, spending time with Viera's nipple. Her other hand slid lower, her hand adding to the sensations between their legs. Viera groaned and trembled with need as nimble fingers played with her clit.

Thorn broke their kiss. "Come on, Viera. Scream for me."

Thorn continued to play Viera like an instrument she'd mastered and Viera forgot how to breathe. She quivered as the heat and pleasure built deep in her gut. Her head dropped and Thorn licked around her ear, nibbling on the lobe. "You're so close, my love. Yell out your release."

Viera's world became Thorn—her hands, her tongue, her words. The pressure within her grew, taking over everything.

"Come for me, love."

Viera's mind fractured. Fireworks exploded and she hollered Thorn's name, collapsing on the other woman.

"Hmmm," Viera moaned a few moments later. "Good morning."

"Morning." Thorn replied, a laugh in her voice.

"Time for my appetizer." Viera pushed herself up and kissed the side of Thorn's neck.

Thorn twined her fingers in Viera's hair. "Not right now. When we get on the ship, we can go to 'bed' early, but we need to meet the others on the promenade soon. You need to go soak. It's better here than on the ship. Make it a double."

Viera sighed. "You're ruining my fun."

A single brow hit Thorn's dark purple hair. "Are you saying you didn't have fun?"

Laughing, Viera pushed herself up. "That's exactly what I'm saying."

Thorn slapped her ass and Viera bit back a moan, thinking how much she enjoyed the other woman's touch as she headed to the closet to gather clothes before her shower and soak.

As always, the promenade was full of beings. The vast number of aliens who came to eat in the social area was the main reason she'd learned how to program the panel to make her own meals. The variety of eating establishments meant that any type of food could probably be found, but Viera didn't speak Galactic Standard and none of the food was familiar to her. On Earth, she was on the short side of average for a human. In the world of aliens, she felt like a halfling.

She and Thorn were the first to the agreed-upon restaurant. A server showed up and Thorn ordered before Viera was required to look over a menu she couldn't read. Once the server left, Thorn smiled sheepishly. "If you don't like what I ordered, we can get something else. I just figured this would be easier."

"What did you get?"

"Eggs, sausage, hash browns, toast, and coffee."

Viera's stomach grumbled in approval. "That sounds amazing."

"I also got a bowl of oats and grain for Flower Prancer. A third plate for Juniper, and a plate of Horax's favorite breakfast. I figure we need to eat fast and get on our way. The crew will transfer our bags so we can leave from here."

Viera slumped in her chair. "Your world is so much more convenient than mine. I can't imagine how hard it was for the chanzii to adapt to the backwater ways of the Earthlings."

Thorn laughed. "It was a bit of an adjustment, but your planet has good points as well. I don't think any of my people have suffered."

Before Viera could respond, Horax lumbered up. "Heya, Thorn, Viera. Good to see you both."

Thorn leaned back as the server brought their drinks. Viera immediately picked up the coffee and brought the mug up to her face. It was hot, but even the scent was fantastic. Thorn asked, "Are you missing any of your training sessions or competition rounds going to Abritos with us? It's four days there, four days back, and several days there on site."

The qynad sighed, lapping up some of his own drink. "I know it's not a short trip, but I don't like you or the ship traveling to a place that could have krottel without me."

Thorn nodded. "I don't think it's necessary. We have several of our ships already there, but I appreciate having you along."

Flower Prancer approached the group, his hooves echoing in the crowded restaurant. *No matter how loud an area is, that Elder always makes himself known.*

"Commander Firoza, qynad, Ms. Kor, are we ready to leave?"

One of Thorn's eyebrows rose. "We just ordered, Elder. I thought we could eat first and then head out. If you've packed, my ship will make sure your items are secured in your rooms."

His tail swished, annoyed as always. "Very well. Where is the server so I can order?"

"I ordered you the standard breakfast. If you don't like it, we can rearrange."

All his motion stopped, and Viera could sense his shock. "No, Commander Firoza, that will be acceptable."

Once their food came, and they'd each taken the edge off their hunger, Flower Prancer shifted his gaze to Viera. "So, Ms. Kor, have you been spending all your time lollygagging about, or have you been at all productive over the last few days?"

Swallowing her bite of sausage, Viera took a sip of coffee while she considered her answer. She wanted to be snarky. *It's my vacation, Elder. I found a beach and sat drinking Mai Tais and eating bonbons. Why? What did you expect?* Biting the inside of her cheek, she took one more sip of coffee to calm herself. "I've spent most of my time practicing magic, if you really want to know."

He made a low grumble in his chest. "Have you figured anything out, Earthling? Or are you still floundering in your studies?"

Viera sighed. "I've figured out how to move the bouncy ball back in time. I had a ven flying around the room and he flew during the magic, so I know the magic was contained."

Another grunt. "Very well. We'll practice on the way to Abritos."

The news wasn't nearly as exciting as the yonat seemed to think it was.

Viera sat on the bed of the room she shared with Thorn on the Ziner. Everyone else, all the important people, were on the bridge, getting the ship moving towards the planet.

As she sat debating what to do, a knock echoed in the room. *How disappointed will the person ... er, being, probably a chanzii, be, when they realize Thorn isn't here?* Grumbling, she opened the door and came face to face with Flower Prancer.

"Ms. Kor, it is time for your lesson. I sent you a message over the computer's system, but you've ignored it. Follow me." He turned and began walking away.

Confused and annoyed, she searched the room for answers before realizing she'd better catch up with the cantankerous yonat.

In the training room, the yonat went to the panel and ordered up a rubber ball: twenty-five centimeters across and purple.

"Ms. Kor, show me this skill you have mastered."

A jittery sensation shivered down her spine. *Why am I nervous? I practiced this for two days. I can do this in my sleep. Okay, not in my sleep, but I know what I'm doing. The magic is mine, it is a well of ability within me, reaching out like invisible tentacles for me to mold and utilize at my will. The mean old unicorn will not intimidate me.* Despite her bravado, her hands trembled as she picked up the ball.

*Okay, Viera, you can do this. Just toss the ball, and back it up in time. Nothing to fret about.*

"Today, Ms. Kor. Neither of us are getting any younger."

It took all her will not to roll her eyes. After taking a calming breath, she tossed the ball. It bounced off the wall with a satisfying thunk. When it was halfway to her, she pushed a bit of her power out to freeze it in time.

"Well, at least you can still do that. From what I can tell, you've isolated only the area around the ball. I'll admit I'm surprised you managed that."

Her ire grew as he spoke, and she used her magic to send the ball back in time. The ball didn't move. She poured a bit more magic into the area. Still, nothing happened.

"Please continue, Ms. Kor. I feel the magic building up but am uncertain as to what you're doing."

She mumbled under her breath. "For fuck's sake." One more push, and she felt her concentration break. There was a loud booming sound before a shock wave of energy slammed both her and Flower Prancer back. The ball, which had been held in stasis, shot forward too fast to see, a purple smudge in the air, and flattened itself on the wall, bits of rubber exploding in every direction.

## Time Keeps On Slipping ... Or Exploding

### Viera

The blast of her spell had driven Viera from the center of the room and into one of the walls. She was thankful she hadn't hit the table. All the air had been forced from her lungs. She wrapped her arms around her legs and rested her forehead on her knees. *What now?*

"Ms. Kor, now is not the time for a nap. You haven't successfully shown me that you can move a ball back in time. We can get the panel to create a new ball. Then we can dissect what happened and figure out what you did wrong."

*Take a nap? What the hell is he thinking?* There were times having an unfeeling teacher may not be the worst thing. She got up and wiped the nonexistent dust from her pants. With a slightly shaky voice she said, "Panel, green bouncy ball, ten inches, if you please."

The ball appeared in the opening, and, trying not to tremble, Viera took it. She closed her eyes and took a few deep breaths. Then she turned and walked confidently to the center of the room. Again, she tossed the ball, waited for the satisfying thunk, and used her magic to stop it.

The ball froze. With a force of will, she ignored anything Flower Prancer had to say. Repeating the motions she'd done over and over in the small guest room in Torville Station Number Six, she pushed out her magic and watched as the ball retreated from her, moving to the wall in the exact arch it had been traveling as it flew towards her.

Once it reached the wall, bounced, and was halfway back to her, she released the magic and let it fly once again, hit the wall, and return to her hands.

"Thank God," she muttered under her breath. Then she turned to her trainer with a smile. "Was that acceptable?"

"Do it again, Ms. Kor." His tone was flat and unimpressed.

Body tense, Viera turned towards the wall and did it again. Everything went smoothly and again she didn't cause a sonic shock wave.

"Again."

The word didn't surprise her this time. His critique of her form did. They spent the next two or so hours moving the ball back and forth in time with Flower Prancer trying to get her annoyed enough to cause a sonic boom, or at least, that's what she assumed.

When the room started to spin, she put her hand on the table and groaned.

"Ms. Kor, have you had anything to eat beyond breakfast?"

She narrowed her eyes at him. "When would I have eaten? You've been with me the whole time."

He grumbled. "Off to the main cafeteria with you. We'll pick this up later. Then we'll discuss that first trick of yours and see if you can master it as well. Though we'll need to get some stronger practice gear."

She couldn't stop the eye roll this time.

The ship served a dish that was similar to pasta, but not quite. It had a green sauce that tasted almost like alfredo but wasn't. There were protein bits that were shaped like meatballs, but ... well, the meal tasted okay, but was weird. The dish was gummy and lacked flavor.

Viera was on her second plate when Thorn sat down next to her. "Oh! Fozzi with narsh, my favorite. The kitchen hasn't made it in forever. They must've gotten the ingredients at Torville Station Number Six." She leaned down, kissed Viera on the cheek, then headed to the kitchen for a plate of food.

When she returned, Juniper and Flower Prancer were with her. They all sat and ate for a few minutes. Then Thorn smiled. "We'll hit the GPS in the middle of the night. You probably won't even feel it. How was your morning? You're eating your fozzi like you like it as much as I do."

There were so many words to sort through. "Flower Prancer found me, and I've been doing magic. I need calories. The food is ... interesting. It's like pasta and meatballs, but not."

Juniper snorted. "That's exactly how Scout first described pasta to me after he tried it. Fozzi with narsh, but not."

A huge smile on her face, Thorn shot a glance at Flower Prancer before focusing on Viera. "So, did you wow with your progress in magic?"

Viera groaned. "I don't think so."

Flower Prancer snuffled and shook his head. "She was adequate. She can move a ball a few seconds back in time, which is a baby step into her magic. She also had a spectacular fail."

Both Thorn's brows flew up. "The fail was that good, eh?"

"She discovered a new magic that we'll need to dissect. If she can recreate it and do it in a secure environment, the failure will be a happy accident. If it was a one-time occurrence, it will be yet another mess up in a long line of my witnessing Ms. Kor not being able to master the simplest aspects of her trade."

Viera bit back the first thing she wanted to say. After working in an elementary school with kids who said mean things and an administrator who was an ass, Flower Prancer was a walk in the park. She slowly set down her fork before it became a 'happy accident' in his face, and asked, "Do you know what magic I performed with my mess up, Elder?"

She tried to sound respectful, but she figured she probably failed when his tail swished.

Like her, he took a moment to eat some food before he answered. *Maybe he needs time to collect himself. Maybe he's only human ... or yonat, or whatever, after all.* "I don't know what it's called. We'll ask around at Torville Station Number Six when we return, but from what it looked like, you sped up the time of the ball itself while slowing down the environment around it. When you released your spell, the ball shot forward like a train, accelerated through space and time, until it hit the wall."

Viera gulped. "It didn't hit the wall, it died against the wall, becoming a pancake of rubber ball. It left an indent."

"Yes, Ms. Kor, that is to be expected at that speed." He was back to being patronizing. Viera felt on better footing with his contempt.

Juniper leaned in. "You know, I have a lot of downtime in the engine room when things are running smoothly, and we have a long trip. I have a few reference books on magic."

Viera perked up at that. She'd been asking for anything she could read, and no one had anything.

Juniper saw her reaction and smiled. "I'll hook you up later, when I have time. The rumors are they don't exist, but it just isn't true. The idea that wizards don't write is ludicrous. They just don't like to share. That's the key you have to remember." She turned back to the yonat. "Anyway, from everything I've read, moving an object in time isn't basic magic. Moving an object in one time frame while the space around it moves in another time is mad skill advanced. You mocking Viera for her lack of anything is rude. You do know that praise helps people learn and advance much better than belittling them, right?"

If it wouldn't have caused a scene, and possibly an international—intergalactic?—incident, Viera would've leapt up and kissed Juniper right then and there. As it was, everyone stared at Flower Prancer, waiting for his answer.

Standing stock still, the yonat snorted. "You are not a trainer, Ensign Snow. You work in the belly of the ship, that is it. I don't tell you how to do your job, you don't tell me how to do mine. Not that you can begin to understand my duties or responsibilities." With a final swish of his tail, he turned to leave. A few steps away, he turned. "Ms. Kor, I expect you in the training room each morning after breakfast. We will figure out your magics on the way to Abritos."

Viera wasn't sure if the words were a promise or a threat. She was just happy to have a few minutes away from her grouchy trainer.

## Another Day, Another Lesson

### Viera

"Again, Ms. Kor."

Viera slowly let out the breath she'd just taken, breathing out the frustration she felt at having spent the last four days with Flower Prancer. She wasn't sure what she'd done to deserve this backlash of karma, but whatever it was, the four days of nonstop training had better be enough to wipe her cosmic slate clean.

She could feel Flower Prancer's amusement. He enjoyed tweaking her. The poor yellow bouncy ball suffered the brunt of her emotional release as she gave it a quick squeeze before tossing it at the wall. With barely a thought, she stopped it, and reversed it back to her hands.

"Now the Sonic Push." His tail swished. *Is he irritated that I'm getting better? Gah! He's so annoying.*

Viera took a few seconds to close her eyes and relax her body and mind before doing magic. Being angry at Flower Prancer was a sure way to mess things up. She had to find her Zen before she did anything harmful. Once she felt she could accomplish what she set out to do, she set down the rubber ball, and picked up a piece of paper.

Over the days they'd been practicing, they'd decided having something that wasn't going to destroy the ship was desirable. She'd discussed the issue with Thorn and Juniper at dinner.

"Why not just use a bouncy ball?"

Viera sighed. "If I generate enough difference between the slow time of the area around the ball and the speed of the area the ball is in, the ball can still explode when it hits the wall. Last time, one of the chunks careened into Flower Prancer."

Juniper bit her bottom lip to stop from laughing.

Thorn's face scrunched up as she thought, in a similar way to Scout. "What about a small metal ball? It shouldn't break apart." She gave a mischievous smile by the end of her statement and she tilted her head in challenge.

Shrugging one shoulder, Viera replied. "It's your ship. If you want all the holes in the wall to repair..."

"Whoa," Juniper leaned forward. "Are the balls moving *that* fast?"

Viera just nodded.

They all ate in silence for a few minutes, then Juniper's face lit up as she stared back and forth between Viera and Thorn. "What about a paper ball? It wouldn't cause damage, and if it *did* fly apart, I doubt it would hurt."

"Today, Ms. Kor, if you please."

Viera shook her head, sad to not be sitting with her friends, and funneled all her angst into crumpling the paper into a ball. She tossed it towards the wall. When it was barely out of her hand, she sped up time for the paper while slowing the time for the air around it. The paper ball existed in a faster time bubble than the area around it, pushing against the static slowed time. This caused a time friction to build, that when all magic was dispersed, allowed the object, the paper, to explode forward like a bullet train.

When she released her magic, the paper zoomed forward, snapping out a sonic blast and the paper ball smacked the wall. *If I added a bit of water, that would be a lot more satisfying.* Viera bit back a snort that threatened to escape her. Explaining the noise to Flower Prancer would probably result in hours more training.

"Adequate. I think—"

The door to the training room opened and Juniper's head appeared. "Sorry to interrupt. It seems the communication panel is down in this room, and you aren't getting our signals from the panel."

Flower Prancer's tail swished. "We are doing significant practice, Ensign Snow. I assume this is important?"

"The Commander requests Viera, er, Ms. Kor on the bridge. We've reached the planet."

Excitement surged through Viera at the thought of finally seeing an alien planet, Thorn's planet. She didn't dart off; she'd been Flower Prancer's student for too long to make that mistake. But when the yonat turned for the door, relief flooded her. *Yes! I can finally be done with his lessons for a bit.*

Though the training rooms were on the lower level of the ship, the lift brought them to the bridge in short order. When the doors slid open, the view screen showed a huge green planet. The sight took Viera's breath away—it was beautiful.

As she slowly stepped forward, her head tilted. "Do you have oceans?"

Behind her, Juniper chuckled. "We do. What you see here is one of our bigger continents. Though Abritos has a lower percentage of ocean coverage than Earth, we do have large water masses."

Viera moved in as close as she could without getting in the way of the crew. "I keep expecting to see cities, like we have on Earth. Do you have anything like that on Abritos? Did the krottel destroy them? It looks like everything on the planet's surface is vegetation."

The more Viera gazed at the planet before her, the more her heart beat faster and numbness traveled down her arms. *What did the bugs do to the planet? Will the chanzii have to rebuild? Has their entire world been annihilated in such a short period of time? Will the bugs try to do the same thing to Earth?* Closing her eyes, she tried to get a fix on the emotions of the others on the bridge. Ironically enough, no one seemed devastated.

She sensed Thorn walk up to her before she felt her warm hand on the center of her back. "No, Viera. The krottel didn't harm our planet, at least, from here it doesn't look like they did. I'd like to get food into you so you're at maximum magical capacity, and then head down to the planet. The ship will do an in-depth sweep and then we'll visit the two biggest cities. I want you to do your mojo thing."

So many thoughts and emotions fought for center stage. Excitement and anxiety were winning out as Viera and most of the bridge crew departed for the cafeteria. Viera wasn't even sure what she ate. All she wanted to do was get down to the planet ... an *alien* planet.

Everyone was a-titter, talking and laughing as they filled plates with food. Many of the chanzii shared stories of their hometowns and what they did before the krottel came.

Learning how to manage and focus her magic took a lot of energy. Everyone knew Viera needed to eat more to balance out what she used by manipulating time. Despite the fact that she wasn't sure what she ate, she did notice that the plate filled up at least once during the boisterous meal.

When everyone was done, they headed to the platform that would transmit them down to the planet. Viera clenched her hands, trying to hide the fact that they trembled. *I'm visiting an alien planet.* She gulped. *Is this really safe? God above, what am I doing?*

Before she could think about it more, she was shuffled up onto the platform with Thorn and Horax and the world started to waver.

## Home Sweet Home

### Thorn

The air smelled ... like home. Chills of excitement ran down Thorn's body as she stood in the pavilion of the main city. The scent of the doxii and frillow—the blue and yellow flowers that decorated the paths—perfumed the air.

Juniper ran over, a tiny squeal following from her throat. "Can you smell them? The flowers? I didn't even realize how much I missed them." She dropped to her knees and picked a yellow frillow, the petals wide and round, and slipped the stem behind her ear.

Thorn knew they needed to get to work, but she wanted to spend a few minutes and let the feel of her world soak into her. The gravity was different than Earth's, Torville Station Number Six's, or even on her ship. The air smelled, even tasted different. The sound of the birds centered her —music that was deeper than the songs on Earth—made her feel relaxed and at home in a way she hadn't in years. Even the low buzz of the insects was familiar.

"I'm finally home," she whispered, her body practically vibrating with its connection to Abritos.

Viera slipped an arm around her. "You are." She leaned in, resting her head on Thorn's shoulder. "Your joy is intoxicating. I feel like I could get drunk on it." The two stood for a few more moments while Thorn let herself enjoy being in such a familiar environment.

After several minutes during which the rest of the bridge crew spent their time walking around, Viera pulled away and looked at where they had landed. "Thorn? You said that the krottel didn't harm your city, right?"

"Yes, that's right."

"And Horax dropped us in one of the major cities that the krottel attacked?" Viera sounded confused.

Thorn took a deep breath, looking over the fields of flowers and trees. There were birds flying in the distance. Flocks of multi-colored flying beasts with flowing silky fur. They were large and friendly, as long as they weren't threatened. The patterns they flew told Thorn the childbearing of the species were near their time. The other three sexes, the two that helped to impregnate, and the one that was the most likely to raise the young, flew and sang the song associated with baby-joy.

Viera leaned in, eyes wide. "Those ... creatures. They are so ... happy." Her eyes widened as she looked at the jestcano grazing in the fields. "Are those walruses?"

Behind them, Juniper laughed. "I was so confused by the similarity of them to our jestcano. Though the beasts look similar, that's where it ends. The jestcano are land beasts with six legs. You can't see it from here. Their smooth hide is actually a bit iridescent, oh, and they lay eggs. Kind of like a turtle, they bury them, but they lay so many, most don't hatch, maybe two in each nest of thirty. It's how they protect themselves. We've developed a way to find the decoy eggs, and it's what we use for cooking and baking."

Viera's mouth gaped open and Thorn wondered if she breathed. After what seemed like too long, she shook her head and huffed out a laugh. "Are there so many of them?"

"Yeah." Thorn nodded. "We prize our open space, so the jestcano run wild. We use sensors to find the eggs so that we don't have to farm them."

"And this is the biggest city?" Viera asked again, the wonder in her voice.

"Yes. This is Traxton, the biggest city on Abritos. It's my home. I was here when the krottel attacked."

Viera slowly turned, gazing at the city. Thorn hoped she thought it was as beautiful as she did. Of course, she couldn't see most of it. The way Abritos built their cities was so different than Earth, it would be interesting to experience it for the first time through Viera's eyes.

"But where is the city? All I see are fields, trees, and some paths. I'm terribly confused." Her eyes were wide as her head swung around. "Everything is amazingly beautiful. And it smells ... are we in a garden? It's so lovely here."

Thorn laughed. Her elation bubbled out of her. "No, this is how it is everywhere on Abritos. We don't build up, Viera, we build down. Come with me." Thorn hooked her arm in Viera's, and they took one of the paths. She pointed. "Do you see the windows over there, the glass roofs? They sparkle all over the field."

After a few steps, Thorn realized Viera wasn't next to her anymore. She turned and Viera stood stock still, jaw dropped, gaping at the field. A moment later, she shook her head. "You build down? Does that mean all your buildings are only one story?"

"No. Only the top floor has the glass ceiling. I'll show you how things on this planet work if you want."

A slow smile replaced the shocked dumbfounded look. She was so adorable. "I'd really like that. Should I be searching for krottel while you give me a tour?"

Leaning down to give her a kiss on her cheek, Thorn said, "That would be lovely." She was so happy about everything.

The two walked down a dirt path. There were some paved paths, but the chanzii honored nature and tried not to disrupt it as much as they could. Viera leaned forward and squinted. "Is that a tunnel?"

"Sort of. Since our homes are built underground, we have our paths underground as well." Thorn led them to the road that would take them to Main Street.

A few feet into the underground street, the walls began to glow. Viera stopped again with a quick intake of breath. "What is that?" She reached out her hand but didn't quite touch the wall.

"We have a multitude of plants, fungi, and plant roots that exhibit bioluminescence. For what feels like all time, the chanzii have built our pathways this way. A lot of our pathways are through natural stone, but some are built through soil that had to be reinforced. Because of all the glowing plants and small insects that live in the soil, there are very few places that need artificial light brought in."

"There are doors and addresses down here!" Viera squealed. "Oh, my God, this is fantastic. How hard was adapting to Earth?" As her head swung around like a bobblehead human, a figurine Thorn could see becoming very popular as a kid's toy, Viera's eyes looked like they may pop out.

Thorn chuckled. "Well, if we want to get mail or packages, it helps if we have an address, and without a door, how will we get into the buildings?"

Viera snorted, then her hands slapped over her mouth. "I'm being dumb. It's just that this is so fantastic and new. It's incredible. My mind is having a hard time keeping up."

"Are you scanning for krottel, too?" Thorn rubbed her back. *Should I be worried about her? I keep forgetting that all of this is new for her. She's impressively laid-back all the time, it's easy to forget that less than a year ago she knew nothing about any of this.*

Viera slid her hand into Thorn's. "I am. I'm not picking up any of the bugs. The city is clear of them."

The two continued to walk through the underground streets. Thorn showed Viera some of her favorite sites. "You'll have to come back once everyone returns. We'll go out to eat, have dessert, maybe visit a game house."

"A ... game house?" Viera sounded confused.

"It's what chanzii do on a typical date. There are many different types of games, physical, similar to your bowling or darts, recreational, like golf or board games, or intellectual, kind of like your escape rooms. Our games are different, but that gives you the idea of our common dates."

"Sounds fun." Viera's eyes twinkled as she continued to take in everything she could from Thorn's favorite city.

## A Whole New World

### Viera

Once Viera understood the size and depth of the city, she realized she'd need the oomph of Gandalf's staff to help her search the city for krottel. She might not really need the staff, but she'd feel better for having the extra focus.

When she closed her eyes and concentrated, she figured she could search an area with a radius of one to two miles. Horax flew out as she used her magic until he was at the edge of her range so they could figure out the distance she could hunt.

The city was huge. Viera wasn't sure if they planned on her walking, or having her send out a pulse, then transport to a new spot to repeat the process again. All she knew for certain was that the area they were in was clear.

Juniper ran up from one of the tunnels ... or underground roads. "Viera, is it hard to continuously scan? Or would it be easier to start and stop?"

Viera scrunched up her face as she thought. "I actually have to work to block my sensing, to be honest. It's my one proficiency that's a bit wild. Since it came from the krottel, it seems to be attracted to them. I think that's why I found the one on the island so easily."

The other woman's eyes widened with her excitement, which washed over Viera. Her head swung around until she found Thorn. "Commander Firoza, I have an idea. Why don't we use the Pedesterizer?"

Thorn's eyebrow rose. "You know, that isn't a bad idea. It's been years. I may be out of shape. We'd need a Double Dome Ped and use two drivers so we could trade off. What do you say, are you up for a drive around the city?"

A smile took over Juniper's face. "You know I am. I'll go dig one out of storage. Be right back."

Watching the Ensign run off, Viera asked, "What is a, um, ped-a-lizer?"

"Pedesterizer? It's the planet's version of a car, or bike, or basic form of transportation. Since we are shapeshifters and honor our sister Abritos, we've never developed technology that harms the planet." Thorn stared at Viera, waiting.

It took a second, but comprehension hit her like the Mack trucks the planets didn't have. "You don't have cars here."

"Nope, or any kind of engine that would pollute the air. We opted for a kind of bike, similar to your elliptical, or stair master. The pedals go up and down. When we need to go anywhere, we hop on, shift our legs to have larger muscles, and go. There are domed versions where a second rider can pedal from the back, and a family-sized vehicle with a dome and two sets of pedals in the front."

The idea of biking everywhere dumbfounded Viera. "You all must be in fantastic shape! I can't imagine going on a family trip and having to pedal the whole way. What if you're going for several hours?"

"Well, we also have transport technology. Many people utilize that daily to get to work or even for basic shopping. We have it all here."

Before Viera could react, Juniper drove up—cycled up? Pedaled up?—in the Double Dome Ped. Thorn opened the back door for Viera; a good thing because she may not have been able to open the door on her own, the controls were not intuitive. The back seat was a comfortable, cushioned bench that went across to the other side. The front had what looked to be two skinny chairs. Juniper straddled the one she'd been sitting on. Thorn adjusted the other to her preferred height, then they were off. For a few moments Viera watched in amazement as Thorn's legs thickened, but then she returned to scanning.

For the next few hours, they took underground roads and above-ground bridges as they crisscrossed all of Traxton. Most of the time, Viera kept her eyes closed, letting her magic run wild. But she made sure to peek out to watch the land pass by. How could she not? They were on an alien planet!

She felt weak and dizzy when they returned to where they'd originally touched down. A full meal had been set out on blankets, and Viera practically fell on the food, shaky and ravenous.

A hand on her arm made her realize others were talking. "I take it you're done for the day?" Viera could feel Thorn's concern.

She swallowed the bite in her mouth and took a sip of, she realized, coffee. The coffee was a balm to her soul. "No, I should be good if you want to do something this afternoon. I just need to keep my calories up."

Flower Prancer, who was there to ensure the krottel were really gone, approached them. "You didn't sense any krottel?"

Viera leaned back on her elbows, finally feeling human again. The thought made her giggle softly to herself. *I'm feeling human on an alien planet speaking to a talking unicorn surrounded by turquoise aliens. Oh, and there's a talking dragon taking care of our logistics. Totally human.* "Not even a twinge."

"Good."

She thought her head might break. *Did he just give me something positive?*

It didn't take long for them to finish eating. They all transported to the far east coast of the continent, to Boullish, the next largest city the bugs had attacked.

The scent of the flowers was still wondrous, but they were different here. There were more purples and blues. The trees had large orange leaves. Others had yellow and green striped leaves the size of what you'd see in the tropics. The temperature was cool, yet the scenery was fantastic.

Something within Viera yearned to spend more time on this planet. The garden-like world of Abritos meshed with her soul. While she connected with ... the magic? The soul? The something ... of the planet, the others found another Double Dome Ped.

Once they found it, the next few hours were a repeat of the morning, down to there being no krottel found.

While they ate under the glow of two of the three moons, Viera couldn't imagine how tired Thorn and Juniper must be. She leaned against Thorn, enjoying the contact.

*I wonder what the three moons are called? What is it like having three moons? And one of them is pink!*

Thorn sipped the wine someone brought down from the Ziner. "If I can get the others to agree, would you like to visit my home, and if it's still in habitable order, stay there with me tonight?"

A warmth blossomed in Viera. "I would like that a lot."

They finished their meal, and Thorn headed off to speak with Horax and the crew of her ship. After several minutes, Thorn returned. "Okay, they're ready to transport us to my home." Her eyes shone, but her hands trembled.

"Are you sure you're ready?"

Thorn bit her bottom lip. "I don't know." She shook out her hands. "I've been dreaming of this day for so long, but what if it's destroyed? What if it's overrun by bugs? What if it's uninhabitable?"

Viera wrapped her arm around Thorn. She was exhausted after their day, but she knew how important all this was to Thorn. "Then we'll figure it out together."

Thorn lived in Roxillion, a town close enough to Traxton she could take a Pedesterizer into the big city for the day if she chose. The day the krottel attacked, she'd transported into the government building to save time. Despite the close proximity, the pedal bikes weren't always more convenient.

When the world stopped wavering and dripping like a watercolor painting, they stood in an underground road. The tunnel system amazed Viera. Riding in the back of the dome bike, she mostly had her eyes closed, searching for the krottel. Thinking of them, she did a quick search ... nothing. Phew!

The walls, ceiling, and floor glowed with lines and specks from the roots, bacteria, and small animal life that emitted a type of bioluminescence. Most was a light blue, almost a cerulean, though some glowed green and light purple. It was bright enough to read by, as long as the typeset wasn't too small.

Each tunnel she'd seen was as wide as the small street she lived on back home on Earth. Barely wide enough for two cars but plenty large enough for the Double Dome Peds. The ceiling wasn't too high, but she couldn't reach it, even if she stood on tiptoe.

She could feel the excitement emanating from Thorn. "God above, Viera, I'm home." Hand trembling, she reached out and tapped a pad by the door. The door slid to the side and a wave of stale air wooshed out. Thorn's hand waved back until she found Viera, and then the two walked in.

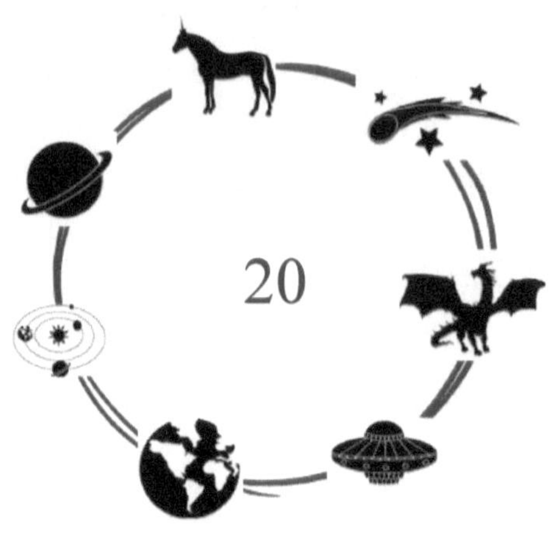

## 20

## An Unexpected Date

### Viera

The first room of Thorn's house was a large open space with a glass ceiling. After years of disuse, the wind had blown dirt, large orange-and-blue-striped leaves, and other natural detritus over the surface. There were small areas of blue sky that peeked in but, for the most part, the room was dark and impenetrable. It smelled a bit stale, like the air hadn't circulated in years ... which it probably hadn't.

"Wait here," Thorn whispered, as if she didn't want to disturb the quiet of the room. Their hands, that had so recently clasped together, slid apart. For a moment, Viera felt alone as she heard Thorn shuffle away, her body nothing but a shadow against the light from the road.

After a few moments, Viera heard tapping. "Panel, bring up lights."

At first, nothing happened. A sense of dread and sadness filled Viera. There had been such hope for this adventure, for Thorn to arrive home and show off what was hers. They'd both known it may not work, but they'd tried to ignore that possibility. Everything else had seemed so promising so far.

The planet was clean of krottel in the two major cities. According to both Thorn and Flower Prancer, that was enough to start moving the ships in that were a few hours out. They'd stayed out of range of the planet so as not to start an accidental war. Now that it seemed the krottel were gone, they could bring the military in and use the high-tech sensors to do a deeper-penetrating sweep for the bugs.

The lights in the room turned on, shocking Viera from her thoughts. "They work!" she said happily. The room was large, similar to a great room on Earth. A large living room area in which Viera could imagine Scout and Thorn spending evenings together, reading and discussing their day. A small dining table adjacent to a kitchen.

Thorn turned to her with a smile. "Yeah. The system had to reboot after being turned off so the krottel couldn't access our technology. I forgot we'd done that." She faced the wall again. "Commander Firoza to the Ziner."

"Ziner here, is your location secure?"

Thorn shot a glance to Viera who nodded. "Affirmative. The panel in the house works and there aren't any krottel within sensory range of Pillar Kor."

"Sounds good. We'll keep an eighteen-hour watch on the coms. If you need anything, someone will be available. Otherwise, enjoy your leave and time at home, Commander Firoza."

"Thanks." She shut off the link and sighed. "Panel, start a cleaning session of the roof."

There were a series of beeps. "Cleaning session has begun."

Thorn's shoulders dropped. "Okay, now that that's done, let me show you my home."

The wall with the panel was across from the main entrance. To the right was a huge room which appeared to be a kitchen, though it wasn't like any on Earth. One counter had a downwards slant, as if it were a sink. Controls like the shower were at one end ... to clean things? There was also a faucet ... for water? There was a peninsula jutting out with seats along one side. A dark panel lay in that counter. *Is that a stove ... or heating unit?*

Thorn moved around touching all the items. "I miss this room almost most of all. I used to cater my baked goods, a bit of savory with the sweet ... I know, you know that, but the thought of making you a meal in my home on my world fills me with such joy. I'm hoping the panel can produce some basic stock items. If not, I'll call the items from the ship."

Viera tilted her head. "The Ziner has a kitchen. Why not cook there?"

Thorn's face contorted and she shook her head. "Up there I'm the Commander. If I'd started making food, people would've lost respect for me. I needed to maintain the air of command."

The pain behind Thorn's words stabbed Viera to her soul. She walked over and enclosed the other woman in a hug, protecting her from anyone who would see her as anything but the wondrous, dynamic, and intelligent beauty she was.

Thorn cupped Viera's face in both her hands and gave her a slow kiss before stepping away. "Okay, now for the rest of the house."

On the other side of the main room, there were several doors along both sides of a wide hallway. The first on the left was Thorn's office. Then a bathroom. The last was Scout's bedroom. Much like his on Earth, it was filled with books and knickknacks of things he loved. Thorn walked in and touched some items. A fuzzy creature Viera didn't recognize, a book, and a figurine. "These were Scout's favorite things. In the rush, he didn't have time to grab them. I should bring back his favorite book and toy, see if he remembers them. I know we're returning soon, but families won't be top of the list, even if I am the Commander."

Slipping up next to her, Viera wrapped an arm around Thorn. "I think that's an excellent idea. Though Scout will be jealous you got to come home, he'll love that he got a piece of his past back."

On the other side of the hallway was the master suite, as they'd call it on Earth. A bedroom/bathroom combination with a huge walk-in closet. The muted earth-tones of light browns, greens, and blues relaxed Viera right away. "I love it!"

The two took a moment to stand and appreciate the room. Thorn sighed. "Okay, I'm going to get some new linens from the panel. If you can make the bed and clean up in here, I'll get dinner made. We have our bags, so if you want to shower, getting a soak wouldn't be a bad idea. There is a layer of magic on Abritos, just not as thick as on Earth. You've done a lot today and you need to replenish."

They embraced before they each went to do their own thing. After her shower, Viera almost melted at the scents floating in from the other side of the house. "God above, that smells divine."

She quickly dressed, finding a black cocktail dress and black flats in her bag. Along the wall between the main room and kitchen was a table. Thorn had set it. Two plates, two water glasses, wine, and candles.

Viera gaped at how beautifully her lover moved in the kitchen as she finished the meal.

"If you could come and find two wine glasses. They're in the cupboard above the sink. I think we'll be ready to eat." Thorn winked as she brought a large dish to the table with something Viera didn't recognize, but her stomach growled, letting her know it very much wanted it.

She found the glasses, and at the table she filled them. They both sat, and Thorn served a pasta-looking meal with a protein.

"What is this?"

"It's Abritos's version of chicken alfredo with steak. Beyond that, it'll take a while to figure out the words to explain the differences."

Two bites in and Viera knew this was beyond better than anything she'd ever eaten. "Marry me!"

Thorn laughed. "Are you talking to me or the food?"

"You know, I don't even know. This is so good."

"Well, let me know once you've decided."

Shock sent tendrils of raw lust through Viera's body at Thorn's words. *Could I really marry Thorn? Would she say yes? Would she want an Earthling?* She gave Thorn a small smile as she continued to eat the mind-blowingly good food.

After dinner, they were both ready to fall over. They had a house and a bed all their own, but after a day of work, cuddling in bed was all either of them could manage. Viera curled into Thorn's arms and quickly fell asleep.

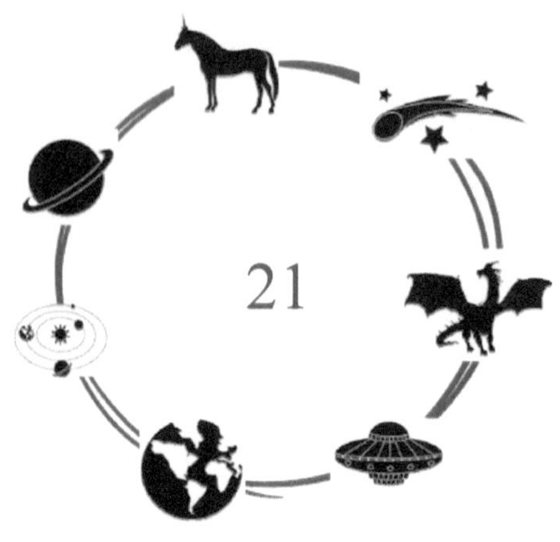

# 21

## There And Back Again

### Viera

Though the ceiling was all windows, there was an optional tinting, that kept the strongest of the morning sun from shining in on Viera and Thorn. When Viera woke up, she lifted up on an elbow and gazed down, admiring how beautiful Thorn was. She traced the other woman's perfect eyebrows down to her soft lips. She leaned down to kiss Thorn's cheek, but at the last moment, the other woman shifted and Viera found herself in a proper good-morning kiss.

Thorn's hands reached up, tangling in Viera's hair. Viera let her hand stroke down the velvet smooth skin until she reached one of Thorn's perfect breasts. She slipped her leg between Thorn's, rubbing their bodies together.

Thorn traced her fingers down Viera's back, feather light, causing Viera to squirm atop her. Viera continued to play with Thorn's nipple as she kissed down to her ear, licking and nibbling the sensitive skin.

Thorn reached Viera's ass, giving it a squeeze, before tracing around to fondle between her legs. Viera bent a knee for better access as Thorn glided her finger over her clit and then in tantalizing circles.

Viera moaned into Thorn's ear. "Yes, give me more," Thorn demanded. "I want to hear you scream my name."

Her finger got more insistent, stimulating Viera. Viera's body trembled as she tried to focus on giving pleasure. The build-up of sensation became too much, and her orgasm exploded out of her in several waves. Beneath her, Thorn groaned in satisfaction.

Once Viera could think again, she tried to initiate more, but Thorn smiled contentedly. "We need to move, love. We can do more on the ride back to Torville Station Number Six, but we're on a tight schedule and I want to show you a few things around my town, and then we need to leave."

Viera sighed, snuggling in closer. "Fine, but I may jump you at any moment. Just be prepared, Commander."

Thorn laughed.

They walked down the street, hand in hand. It didn't take long for the tunnel to dump them back out at an outdoor train. Knowing what Flower Prancer expected, and what she hadn't done, Viera picked up a stone. With a bit of focus, she gave the small pebble a toss and played with the time around it and for it. Once she released the magic, it shot off, zooming through the air like a rocket.

Both she and Thorn gaped at how far and fast it went. Thorn finally turned her stunned face to her. "You didn't know it would do that?"

"No. I've been practicing on the ship with paper. I had no idea." Tingles of apprehension danced across her body.

Thorn shook her head in apparent shock. "It was awesome and terrifying, you know that, right?"

"I agree."

Thorn reached down and picked up a few more pebbles. "Can you do it again?"

"Do you really want me to?" The idea dumbfounded Viera.

"You can only use what you can master."

Viera laughed, disrupting some birds in a tree. "Did you get that from Flower Prancer?"

Thorn snorted. "No. Actually, Betsy, if you must know."

Viera took another pebble and repeated her actions. The same thing happened. Thorn had a far-off look. "What if I threw the stone? Could you do the same thing then?"

"Don't know, but I don't see why not?"

Thorn tossed the next pebble, and Viera performed the sonic toss, as she was coming to think of it, rocketing it off down the field.

A land bridge, a path over a part of the field that Thorn explained was a path for animals, came up in front of them. Excitement filled Thorn to the point Viera could sense it. "Just over this bridge is my bakery. I want to show it to you, and then we can return to the ship."

Viera reached out and took her hand. "You say that like I haven't completely enjoyed myself. I'd stay here as long as you wanted."

Thorn turned away, but Viera thought she heard her say, "Not as long as I really want you to stay."

The four-day journey back to Torville Station Number Six was much like the one to the planet. Most of the crew were busy making the Ziner run smoothly. Flower Prancer insisted that Viera spend her time practicing her magic.

The only benefit was that they finally moved on to a variety of magics. Time was off the table.

Viera did pounce on Thorn when she wasn't expecting it, but she waited until they were alone in their room. She thought a show on the bridge may have been a bit flashy for both of them.

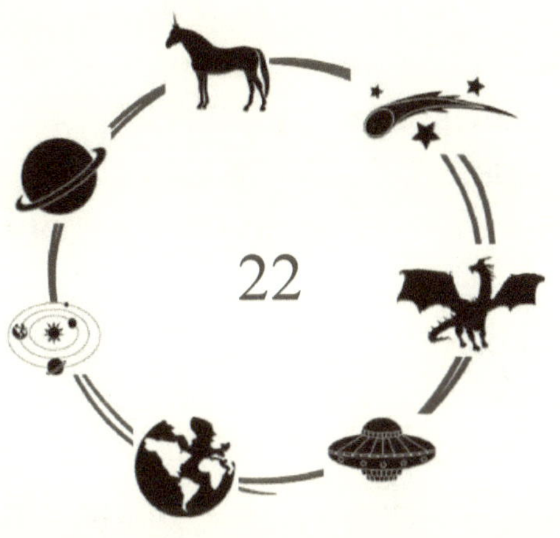

# Tying Up Loose Ends

## Betsy

The sound of the two ven knocking over Betsy's suitcase woke her up. *Fucking flying cats! Why the hell did I want the beasts?*

Buttercup flew and landed next to her, rubbing her soft, furry face against Betsy's hand as she made a low sound, similar to a purr, that meant she was happy. With an exaggerated sigh, Betsy scratched the miscreant pest until it quivered beneath her ministrations.

From out of nowhere, Westley landed on Betsy's hip, demanding his turn. Betsy shifted her attention from the gray beasty almost asleep next to her, to the devil, almost all black, prancing up and down her side. Wes, as she thought of him, had a heart of gold once he settled down, but he loved to play.

She'd taken to waking up twenty to thirty minutes early each day just to have some time to give the two ven some attention.

Though Wes loved the scritches, he soon was off, flying around. He loved to be the void in flight, the shadow that zoomed, darkness before the nap. That was Betsy's cue to rise and get them all food.

Once her flying friends were munching, she grabbed a pair of jeans and a long-sleeved T-shirt with a large pineapple on it and headed for the bathroom. After a quick shower and a double dose of soaking, she dressed.

Being off-planet always made her feel weird. The high concentration of magic on Earth wasn't needed for a wizard, but it meant her body was used to the higher levels, almost like an addiction. Being off-planet felt like she was in magic withdrawal.

Once she was sure the ven were okay, she slipped out of her room and headed to find Scout. She signaled her arrival on his door pad. A moment later, he opened the door looking bright-eyed and ready for the day. "Hi, Pillar Doeth. How are the ven this morning? Do they miss their siblings?"

Betsy smiled at his exuberance. His words tumbled from his mouth so fast. "They're doing great. They've taken over my small room and I'm sure once we're back on Earth, they'll love my home. It's big enough for them and I have a large wooded area where they can fly free and explore."

He beamed. "Can I come and visit them there?"

"Of course. But we're getting ahead of ourselves. Let's start with today and breakfast."

The glow and energy seemed to seep out of him. "It's Tiffany's last day, you know. Her parents found a ship that will take them back to her planet and it leaves today."

The two of them walked to the dining area. "I heard." Betsy reached down to take his hand and give it a squeeze. "I know you're going to miss her, but it'll be good for her to be with her own people. You like being with the chanzii, right? You wouldn't want to be left alone on Earth without everyone else, would you?"

Scout's face scrunched up as he thought about her words. "No, I guess not. I'm just going to miss my friend, that's all. I'm tired of missing people. So many people from Roxillion—that's the place Mom and I used to live—they didn't end up on Earth. Most of my friends ended up on a planet that knows about us, and spaceships, and aliens and, well, everything. I've kept in touch some, but it's hard. It'll be hard losing Tiffany, too." His chin dropped to his chest as he finished speaking.

Betsy stopped walking to kneel next to him. She pulled him into a hug, holding him tight. "Oh, Scout! So much for someone so young. You'll be able to message Tiffany, even if you don't see her every day. And if your Mom is right and the krottel are gone, you'll be heading home sooner than everyone thought. Maybe even in a year or so."

His body tightened. "Why so long? Why not now?"

Betsy sighed. "Once the planet is clear of the others, it has to be rebuilt. Groups will go to make sure it's safe. Then your people will be brought back in waves. Also, if all the chanzii leave Earth at the same time, it'll cause a big stir on my planet. It may happen in less time, I just don't know."

To Betsy's utter shock, Scout started to laugh. "Can you imagine, all of the chanzii communities suddenly deserted? Your people would freak out. The stories they'd tell would be amazing."

She laughed with him. He wasn't wrong. The conspiracy theorists would create more sordid tales about a series of towns all over the world suddenly empty overnight than even she could clean up. "So, you see," she said, "it has to be gradual."

Scout nodded. "Yeah, you're right. And since Mom is the Commander, we're probably going to be there until the end." He shook his head. "Do you know when she'll be back?"

Since she'd taken charge of the boy, she'd learned to just go with his change of subject and switch of emotions. "I don't. They left six days ago, and the trip is four days, Abritos time. But Abritos has an eighteen-hour day, which is equivalent to twenty-six Earth hours. Torville Station Number Six has a day equivalent to thirty Earth hours, so ... gah! They've been away about seven of your planet's days. If it took four days there. Two to three days on planet. You know, they may be on their way back. I'll try to contact them after breakfast. A call from her son may not go over well on the bridge, but a call from a Pillar sounds official."

As she spoke and did her calculations his face scrunched up. "Why can't everything just be the same? It would be so much easier!"

She tapped his nose. "I agree. Now, breakfast?"

He nodded, and they continued their trek.

In the dining hall, they each ordered up a meal. They were early and most of the room was empty. Betsy took her bagel with cream cheese and a large coffee to a table. Scout had a bowl of cereal and a glass of juice. After returning with her second mug of coffee, Betsy found Tiffany and her parents had joined them.

"Hi. I hear today is the day. When does your transport leave?" Betsy watched as the two kids talked animatedly at the far end of their table.

Tiffany's dad stared at Betsy for a few moments. Neither of Tiffany's parents much liked any of the adults on the ship. For some reason, they believed everyone was against them. It wasn't true; no one gave them much thought when they weren't around. A serious case of 'out of sight, out of mind.' But it would be rude to say that to them.

With a huff, the man finally spoke. "We leave in two hours. We're all packed, and in a couple of days, we'll finally be home. Our families are thrilled that we've escaped that backwater planet of yours."

*And they wonder why people avoid conversations with them.*

Betsy managed a tight smile. "I'm glad everything has worked out then. Is it okay for Scout to hang out with Tiffany for her last hours on the station, or would you rather not?"

His face screwed up to spit out some vitriolic answer, but before he could, his wife sighed, shaking her head. "It's fine. He's her only friend and I want her to have good memories and an easy transition. If we say 'no,' I fear she'll be in tears for days. I'm starting to figure out what living with a teen is going to be like."

Betsy's smile softened. "A common complaint I hear from parents." She saw from the tightening of both adults' faces, she'd used the wrong words. Before they could snap, she held up a hand. "I'll be at the launch in an hour and a half to collect Scout. Until then, I need to make some official communications."

They both looked at her hand, then snapped their gazes away. She was dismissed. Betsy rolled her eyes as she collected her dishes. She dropped a kiss on Scout's cheek. "You can hang out with Tiffany until she boards her ship in an hour and a half. I'll see you then. Okay, champ?"

If his smile was a bit sad, she thought—hoped—she was the only one to notice.

Betsy sat at a small desk in the room she'd been assigned. First on her list, she sent a message to the bridge of the Ziner requesting a meeting with Thorn and whomever else the Commander thought would be appropriate.

Once that was complete, Betsy ordered a mug of hot chocolate with marshmallows while she waited for the reply. She was about to open a book, when a response popped up on her screen. "Pillar Doeth, we'd appreciate a meeting in ten minutes."

The time slipped by, and the meeting started. When Betsy entered the virtual room—a virtual reality of a room with a table and chairs for each of them to sit at—she found Thorn, Horax, Major Shifts, and Violet North. Betsy checked her watch. *It's like eight at night on the West coast ... okay, not too bad.* A small thrill buzzed through her at the sight of the other chanzii.

"Our trip to Abritos was ..." Both Major Shirts and Violet leaned forward as Thorn spoke. She shook her head as she searched for words. "I can't even explain how my soul sang at being home." She looked down, maybe checking over notes. "Pillar Kor did an in-depth search for the krottel in Traxton and Boullish. We figure if there are any krottel left, that's where they'd be. She didn't find any. Major, I want to bring in three ships and do a full localized scan of the planet. We've done the distance scans, but with the cities with distance-weapon capability clear of the bugs, we can bring our ships in."

Major Shifts's smile was infectious. Betsy couldn't help but to smile back at him. His eyes twinkled. "These are some of my favorite orders you've given, Commander Firoza. I'll get the ships in position by the end of day today. The scan will take three days to be thorough. If our assumptions, hopes, and dreams are correct, what's the next move?"

Thorn's face was just as gleeful as the Major's. "We bring in the builders. I want crews everywhere. It will take a few months, but without people living on-world, it should be easier. As locations get cleared for residents, we move our people back."

As if he recognized Thorn's voice, Wes woke up from his multi-hour nap Betsy had hoped would continue and launched himself to her shoulder. One of his wings covered her eyes for a moment before he settled.

A grumble came over the meeting's speaker as Thorn admonished, "Betsy, you're being attacked by a vicious ven."

Horax's low voice chuckled. "I think the black menace is adorable. I'd fly with him."

Betsy scoffed. "I thought you were happy I took two from your stable. You still have four in your unit, unless Tiffany takes one when she heads home today."

Wes made his happy purring sound, his antenna bobbing just to the left of her peripheral vision. As cold as the station was, the extra body heat wasn't the worst thing.

Before Thorn could make another anti-ven comment, Violet's brows came together. "Not that I don't love being in on this discussion, Commander Firoza, but why am I here?"

Thorn's face hardened. "I want to be on Abritos overseeing everything during this transition. I've been the face of this since the start, and I want to see it to the end. I want to ensure our people have the home they've been dreaming about. If I'm leaving Earth, I need you to take over as the leader of the chanzii on Earth. Since you know Pillar Doeth, you'll be working with her."

Violet's eyes darted to Betsy's and she gave a quick smile. *Is she blushing? Or am I projecting?* "I can do that, Commander Firoza." Her eyes shot back to Betsy. "I'm your woman."

As they continued to plan their next moves, Betsy contemplated the tiny thrill she felt at the thought of working with Violet.

## The Journey Home

### Viera

**I** can't believe Torville Station Number Six is starting to feel like a version of coming home." Viera bit her lip. "Not that I didn't love Abritos, it's just ..."

Thorn wrapped her arms around Viera from behind. "I know what you mean. The station feels familiar to me as well. Don't get me wrong, I would've stayed on Abritos if that was possible, if more of my people were there," she paused for a few moments and then squeezed gently, "if you were there with me. You know, things that were familiar. But it's too soon."

Viera spun in Thorn's arms. "Would you want me on Abritos? A gangly human who's too weak to use your basic transport system?"

Thorn leaned down to kiss her softly. "I find that I'm addicted to you, my *gangly human*. And I happen to know my son loves you as well. So, yes, I feel that home and you are pretty synonymous at this point. But I know how it feels to be taken from your home planet, so though I'm telling you this, don't respond. Not without thinking about it. This is a big decision. Just know, either way, I love you, Viera Kor, Pillar of Earth."

Warmth and chills flowed through Viera's body in waves. She clasped her hands behind Thorn's neck, pressing her body against the woman she'd fantasized about until the day she landed in her arms. She couldn't imagine feeling this way about anyone else. Lifting up to her toes, she kissed Thorn back, just as tender. "I have so many words I want to say back to you. I'm filled with a novel of thoughts ... a series of novels of words for you, but we're about to dock, and I don't have the time. And

I know I'm babbling now, and I fear it'll just get worse." She squeezed her eyes shut, then took a breath before looking up at Thorn's jewel-green eyes. "Just know, I love you, too."

When the door between the Ziner and Torville Station Number Six opened, Scout ran in and leapt into his mom's arms. Viera could feel the joy pouring off both of them.

Once Thorn put him down, he turned to Viera, and his emotions dropped. His sadness washed over her. He trudged over to her. "Ms. Kor, Tiffany's gone."

She dropped to her knees and gave him a hug. "Oh, sweetie. I know you two were good friends. I'm sure you can still message her."

"I know, but I miss her. And it'll take so long until I can go home ... you know, my *real* home, Abritos. But not forever, so why make new friends on Earth? It'll just end like Tiffany. It's all awful. I just want friends to grow up with."

She hugged him tighter. "Can I be your friend?"

He sniffled. "But you're an adult. And when we leave Earth, you'll stay there, so you're like the rest, aren't you?"

She smiled at him. "I know, but we can still be friends until you leave, can't we?"

He wiped his nose on his arm. "I guess."

Behind him Betsy put her hands on his shoulders. "I know he seems broken up, but believe me, we had some good times while you all were gone."

He looked up at her. "Well, that's true. We did. Tiffany just left a few days ago, and Betsy was great." He sniffed. "I'm sorry, Ms. Kor. I just miss people."

She gave him another hug before standing up.

Thorn's face was soft as she watched them. "Okay, bud. We're going to pack and head back to Earth. How much time do you need?"

"I'm ready to go now. Well, no ... maybe a half-hour?"

Betsy ruffled his hair. "Well, I need about an hour." She shook her head. "That is, unless that rascal, Wes, has messed up my room again."

Thorn threw her head back and laughed. "No take-backsies. You asked for the ven, now they're yours."

The group turned to their rooms, but before they got far, Balzeno approached. "Earthling, Pillar Viera Kor, I am glad to have run into you. Are you planning to stay on the station for a few days?"

Tingles of shock prickled up and down Viera's body. She licked her lip, dry from shock that the dwarf had acknowledged her again. "Um, sir, er, Elder Balzeno. No, I'm afraid not. We need to get back to Earth. We're just here to pack and pick up the crew who didn't travel to Abritos with us."

One of his bushy brows quirked up a pinch and he smiled slightly. "Very well. We'll have to find another time to talk. Maybe I'll visit that magical planet of yours. Until then, I have a gift for you. With your trifecta of powers, making you the youngest Elder ever, I know that your magic is hard to contain. Time is a tricky proficiency. I've created this bauble for you. I hope you'll accept it."

He held out a small silver bracelet, simple, but elegant. It was made of two intertwined bands. Where they crossed there were tiny leaves or flowers all in silver. In the center of each flower was a small amethyst.

Viera held her hand as stable as she could to take the beautiful trinket. Before she could grab it, Balzeno slipped the bracelet on her wrist and clasped it shut. Viera could feel the magic pulsing through the metal, though she had no idea what it did. Apprehension filled her. "Thank you."

"May time always be on your side, my dear." He winked, then spun on his heel and sauntered off.

Behind her, Flower Prancer snuffled. "Ms. Kor, we'll need to figure out the magic in that artifact. Meet me in the training room in two hours."

She groaned as she headed off to pack.

It didn't take Viera long to get the things on Torville Station Number Six packed. Most of her belongings were already on the Ziner. Once she was done with her stuff, she helped Scout with the ven and Thorn with her stuff.

When they got to the ship, she and Thorn went to their room to unpack. "Do you think Scout will be okay?"

Thorn sat on the edge of the bed. "I think so." She leaned back on her hands. "He's been moved around a lot." She let her head fall back as she thought. "I'll tell him when we get home and things get finalized that we're heading back ... home. He'll be happy to know we're taking this final jump." She shook her head. "Deciding to have Violet take over on Earth so we could return to Abritos was the right decision but it's suddenly all happening so fast. I may need to find some of his old friends and their families and get them on the short list to return. I don't want him to be lonely."

Viera leaned against the wall. "So, he'll come home with you. What will he do during the day?" As excited as she was for Thorn and Scout, the realization that this was the beginning of the end felt like she'd been hit with a ton of bricks.

She sighed. "I don't know yet, but I don't want him to be on Earth alone. He needs to be with me. There are probably other workers with kids who will be coming to help rebuild. He won't be alone."

"Okay, yeah. With the transporters, the kids can all be corralled during the day. It should be manageable." Viera's mind started putting the pieces together for a world so unlike her own.

Before anything else could be said, an alarm came from the panel. Viera tapped on the wall. "Ms. Kor, it has been two hours and three minutes. You're late."

Viera bit back a groan and Thorn covered her mouth as she chuckled. Viera plastered a smile on her face. Her mom always said a smile could be heard over a phone line; this was probably the same thing ... right? "Sorry, on my way."

With a wave, she headed out the door and ran. The urgency in her had her running faster than she'd ever run before. There were a few people in the halls, but they were just standing still, probably checking out a data pad or something on a panel display. She didn't spend time analyzing as she made her way to the training room at top speed.

She burst into the room to find Flower Prancer backing up from the panel. His violet eyes snapped to her. "Ms. Kor, you're here."

"Well, yeah. You just snapped at me for being late. Why wouldn't I be here?"

"I just messaged you, Ms. Kor. It's been mere seconds. Did you have Horax or Ensign Snow transmit you down here?"

The familiar sensation of frustration bubbled in her. "Of course not. I just ran. You made it sound important, though with days of travel and nothing to do but train, I don't know what a few minutes matter." She took a deliberate breath to calm herself. "But no, I just ran."

His voice flat with disbelief, he said, "That's impossible, no one runs that fast."

She clenched her jaw for a moment. "I passed people in the hallway, Elder."

His eyes narrowed before he stepped back and shook his head. Then his eyes lowered to the bracelet. "Do you feel winded? Sore?"

Viera paused, realizing she didn't. She felt a bit nauseous, but beyond that, the run didn't feel any different than if she'd walked to the room in an easy saunter. She lifted her arm to gaze at the bracelet. "I think you may be right. I need to know what this bracelet is doing to me."

It took most of the trip to the GPS and beyond to figure out how the bracelet controlled her super-speed. The ship wasn't the best place to learn its features. Viera also realized it helped her control other aspects of time magic.

When she went to shower, she couldn't figure out how to take it off, and neither could Thorn, so it stayed on. One day when she met the dwarf again, she'd have a list of questions a mile long.

After the Ziner passed through the GPS, the krottel ship was spotted near Earth. Two messages were sent, but true to form, they didn't respond. When they got close enough to confirm the ship was within a day's travel to Earth, Thorn sent a message to Earth warning them. Viera hoped they had their sensors listening for incoming messages. They hadn't thought the krottel were anything to worry about, but the ship on their sensors told a very different story.

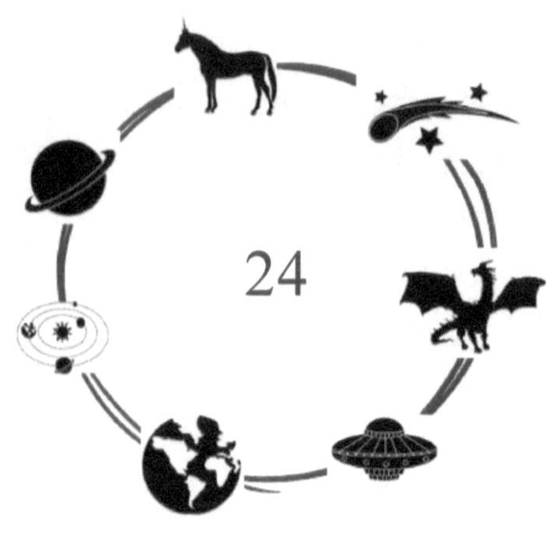

## We Come In Peace ...

### Viera

As the Ziner approached the krottel ship, Flower Prancer, Viera, and Juniper headed up to the bridge. Betsy was already there. They all sat at a table in an alcove out of the way of the bridge crew. Viera watched as the krottel ship grew in the display, outpacing the size of Earth.

Trembling, Viera whispered. "There are so many bugs on that ship."

Flower Prancer gazed at her. "Ms. Kor, we are far from them. Are you saying you can feel them?"

She realized her nails bit into the palms of both hands and tried to relax. "It's like ... we know they're a collective with a queen, or several queens. Because they pushed their sensing magic into me, I'm somehow still—" a shiver ran down her back, "—I don't know."

Thorn looked at her; concern radiated from her. "Do you think they can sense you as well? Do they know you're here?"

Viera shook her head. "I don't think they care. I'd be like one of the drones, not nearly important enough to be picked up individually."

Horax rumbled, "Are you sure? You know I care for the safely of this vessel, but you're a friend, and I care about you too. I'll fly you away from here to someplace they can't find you, Viera, just say the word."

She smiled. "Thank you, Horax. I know you would."

Once everyone knew she was okay, they went back to monitoring the ship. It was definitely on a direct line to Earth. Flower Pracer moved towards the center of the bridge. "Let me send another message to them."

Thorn sighed. "We've tried sending them messages. What makes you think this time will be different?"

"Commander Firoza, before they were a ship in space. Now they are approaching a planet the Elders specifically told them to avoid. Please open a channel."

She narrowed her eyes and shook her head. "Comm, open a channel. Let the Elder have his say."

Horax, near the front of the bridge, grumbled low, "You can speak ... now." He tapped the console with his large paw. The qynad moved with grace and finesse.

"Krottel. This is Elder Flower Prancer, ambassador of the yonat to the chanzii living on Earth and the Earth Pillars. In our last meeting, you were told to not enter this space or approach Earth. The people of this planet don't know about other alien species yet. The magic of their world and their planet in general is off-limits to you. Stop your approach and respond to this communication."

A tension grew on the bridge. The feelings tingled along Viera's skin as everyone waited for a response. She could almost hear their thoughts as people knew nothing would come from Flower Prancer's words.

Thorn stood, a stiffness in her body, ready to give a command for action. Before she could say a word, Flower Prancer's tail switched. Viera recognized his sign of annoyance; she saw it often enough.

His head turned from the display, which hadn't changed. "I will take a small ship over and demand a conversation with them. They can't ignore me if we're standing face to face."

"Not that you're really speaking to their faces," Thorn mumbled softly, barely loud enough to go further than where Viera sat.

Flower Prancer's violet eyes narrowed, but before he could snap at her, Juniper cleared her throat. "I don't think that's a good idea. We don't know why they're not responding. I don't like it. It's not safe for you to go, Elder. I will go."

He snorted. "Who are you, Ensign? When you get there, they'll laugh in your face."

"They don't know anything about any of us. They don't know me from Commander Firoza. All we know is that they've been ignoring us. We just need someone on that ship to find out why. In the end, I'm the most expendable, and you know that. As you said, who am I? I'm the one the ship needs least."

It felt like someone had punched Viera in the gut. *How can she think that of herself? Every person on this ship is very needed.*

"Very well, Ensign Snow. Take the small one-person shuttle and find out why they're ignoring us."

Thorn rubbed her eyes. "If you don't mind, Elder, I'd like to make final decisions since, you know, I'm the Commander of this ship."

Flower Prancer had the decency to look a bit abashed. "My pardon, Commander Firoza. As you see fit."

She sighed. "Ensign Snow, I don't like sending anyone, but you know that small boat better than anyone on the ship. If anyone is going to fly it over to the krottel and back safely, it's you. It's not that you're the least needed, it's that you have the best skills for the job. You're a valuable member of my crew. Don't forget that."

Juniper smiled shyly, ducking her head. "Thank you, Commander Firoza. I'll head down to the shuttle bay. I'll call up when I'm ready to head out."

"Sounds good, Ensign." Thorn nodded curtly and watched her as she headed to the lift. Viera observed them both, feeling Juniper's excitement and Thorn's resignation.

After a few minutes, Juniper's call came up, and they all viewed as the image of the shuttle left their ship. It looked so small in comparison to the krottel's behemoth of a machine. It was almost like Juniper became the bug approaching the monster.

As she watched, Viera stood. She realized she held the walking stick as the cool metal of the bracelet slid down her arm. The heft of the time-piece weighed heavy in her pocket. She wasn't sure why all her magical implements wanted to make themselves known to her, but they all battled in her mind, subconsciously saying, 'hi.'

Step by step, apprehension gripped her as the small shuttle got closer and closer to the larger silent beast. Her heart beat faster and her empty hand trembled. Sounds faded around her as her whole focus, her whole being, became Juniper and the krottel. *What am I missing?*

Suddenly, as if someone had turned on the television in her mind, she knew. She saw it clear as day. The premonition came to her in hi-definition, full color, full emotion, reality.

"No!"

It occurred to her she yelled into the quiet of the bridge. No one else saw the krottel obliterating the small ship in a fireball no one could survive.

Viera held out her hand and tried to stop what she just saw. Space was big ... so big. The shuttle was small, but larger than the ten-inch green bouncy ball. The watch in her pocket heated up; she funneled more magic through the walking stick. She hoped the bracelet would amplify anything she had.

Space was so gigantic.

The krottel ship was enormous.

She pushed more magic out, as much as she could muster.

The beam of energy shot from the krottel ship.

*More, I have to have more magic. Stop! I have to stop that beam!* Tears fell from her eyes.

Her vision darkened as she saw the laser continue on its path. Viera tried to push out more magic. She heard voices around her right before her vision blackened and something cold hit her arm and then the side of her head.

## We Know Best ... Ladies

### Betsy

The drive to Thorn's house was familiar after the years she'd lived on Earth. Betsy knew the time was coming to an end now that Abritos was free of the krottel that apparently orbited above their heads. After the destruction of Juniper's shuttle, it took every bit of diplomatic training she and Flower Prancer had to stop Thorn from starting a war right there in the dark space above Australia.

A full crew was left on the ship, though several people headed back down to the planet. If Betsy were to guess, Earth was in more danger than the Ziner.

Thorn had demanded Viera be taken to her house to recover after her collapse. Though Betsy had thought she'd heard some whisper of her friend's turmoil in her mind before the collapse, Flower Prancer had heard more of it. Their closer working and similar magic types had created a bond that Viera probably wouldn't be happy to know existed.

Viera's outburst before she threw up a hand and poured every bit of magic she had out into the vast emptiness of space was enough to let Betsy piece together that she'd seen the explosion in a premonition before it had happened. A baby in the world of magic, even a seasoned warrior would have a hard time affecting that much volume of ship, space, and time. Viera was lucky to have survived the attempt.

Betsy wanted to arrange a meeting with Juk, their wayward youngling of a government official out in New York, to discuss the krottel ship just a bit further out and hiding behind the moon. She hoped that this time the powers-that-be would listen, but she wasn't holding her breath. As she parked in front of Thorn's house and headed up to the front door, she also yearned for her friend to be okay. Not only did she want Viera to be awake, she wanted her friend to be feeling better. The chanzii had a higher appreciation for life than the people of Earth, or so it seemed, so she knew Viera had been in good hands. Viera and Juniper had been friends. Betsy wanted Viera to head into this meeting with her, but she wouldn't push.

The door opened quickly after she knocked. Scout gazed up, his green eyes bright. "Hi, Ms. Doeth. How are Buttercup and Westley?"

He stepped back, letting Betsy enter. "They are doing well, though Wes ... Westley, is a scamp. He's always getting into trouble."

Scout snickered. "Mom was rather happy when she heard it was those two you were taking."

From the back of the house, Thorn's voice echoed, "What was that?"

Scout ran halfway down the hall and yelled, "Nothing, Mom! We're talking about the ven."

Thorn's sigh was loud enough the neighbors could probably hear it. "Send Betsy to my room, dear."

Scout led the way, though Betsy knew the layout of the house well enough. In Thorn's room, Viera lay in the bed, eyes shut. Betsy placed a hand on her forehead. She felt fine. "Has she woken up since she passed out yesterday?"

"No. She's just slept the whole time. Should we get a doctor?" Thorn pulled a chair up and sat, clasping Viera's hand in hers. She gnawed on her lower lip, obviously worried.

Betsy sat on the side of the bed. She hadn't done much healing or magical mojo, but she'd studied the theory with her father and some of the other Pillars. Viera was drained, and probably depressed. "Can you get a cup of coffee and something she can eat? If I can wake her up, she's going to need both."

Thorn nodded and headed out.

"Okay, Viera, here goes nothing." Betsy placed one hand on Viera's chest, the other on her forehead. She closed her eyes and imagined her magic was a river. *All I need to do is push a bit of my river over a waterfall into Viera. Not a lot, just enough for her to wake up and start to build up her own reserves.*

She imagined a slow trickle of her magic dripping down from her into Viera. Betsy breathed slowly and deliberately, her body trembling with the effort of siphoning the magic away. The process was anathema to everything she'd learned. Her reservoir of magic was vast, she had plenty to give, but the idea was just plain weird.

After what felt like hours, but was probably only a minute or so, Betsy heard a stuttering breath. The muscles under Betsy's hand tensed then trembled. "Betsy? What are you doing?"

With a sigh, Betsy pulled back and opened her eyes, smiling down at her friend. "Look at you, being awake and stuff. How do you feel?"

"Tired. Weak. Shaky." She squeezed her eyes shut. "You wouldn't happen to have coffee? Do you?" Her tone was so hopeful, a smile spread across Betsy's face. "Wait, where am I? And why are you here?"

"She doesn't, but I do," Thorn said from the doorway. "You don't know how thrilled I am that you're awake."

Viera tried to sit but failed. Betsy took the items Thorn carried so she could slip in behind Viera, helping her up. Then Betsy gave her the coffee first. Viera groaned in appreciation.

Once Viera had enough in her to sit on her own, she looked around the room. "We're not on the ship, but my last memories ... they aren't a nightmare, are they?"

Betsy shook her head. "No, they aren't."

"Are the damn bugs attacking here, then? Do you need me at top magical ability? I'll fight, even if it's just throwing rocks."

Betsy's shoulders drooped, though she saw Thorn smile at that comment. At least that wasn't where they were. "No, but I ... we, if you want to join me, have a meeting with the government officials in an hour. Mr. Juk Hopkins himself."

"Last time it took a few days to get a meeting. How did you get one so quickly this time?" Viera sounded impressed.

"Oh! I haven't called him yet. Shall I do that now? I wanted to make sure you'd be up for the meeting before I called."

Viera smiled. "Yeah, let's see how much time I have to shower. I may want to head up to the ship and take a soak or five."

Thorn slapped her forehead. "For fuck's sake, I should've done that, shouldn't I? It would've helped, right?"

Betsy shrugged. "Maybe. I'm surprised Flower Prancer didn't mention it."

Viera rolled her eyes at the mention of her trainer.

Pulling out her phone, Betsy dialed Juk's direct phone number. "Hello?" His young voice sounded almost professional. "Juk Hopkins."

The hesitancy of his voice made Betsy smirk. She didn't know why his boss assigned such a young pup, except that they must have known it didn't matter. They were all young pups to her. "Hi, Mr. Hopkins. It's Betsy Doeth. Viera Kor and I need to come in and speak with you today. We can be there in an hour or two, whichever works better for you."

The poor boy sputtered for a full minute before he could get words out. "Ms. Doeth, how did you get my direct number? I didn't even know I had a direct office number."

"You read my files, Mr. Hopkins. Let's not back-slide. This is important. One hour or two?" She tried to be succinct, but worried she'd have to go over his head again.

"You don't understand. I'm busy. I couldn't meet with you for at least a week." She could hear papers and typing in the background as he floundered.

"That won't work. Two choices. One hour or two." Her voice had hardened. After this event, she was going to go to his boss and get a better point-person. She deserved better than this.

"I just don't know if that's possible, Ms. Doeth. Is it a matter of national security?"

She sighed. "Mr. Hopkins. Are you going to give me a time to meet? One hour or two? If not, the decision *will* be made for you. Remember what happened to your predecessor."

He laughed ... *laughed.* "Oh, Ms. Doeth, I'm not worried about that. Next time, call by proper channels. I can talk to my aide, and we can find a time next week. Maybe next week Thursday?"

Betsy hung up. "Go up to the ship, shower and soak. Come back for breakfast. I'll get this meeting arranged." She knew she sounded annoyed. But someone in New York was about to be much more annoyed.

Viera gathered an outfit, grabbed her coffee, then went to the panel and requested a direct transmit to Thorn's room on the Ziner. Thorn went with her.

Once they were gone, Betsy found the number for Orson Mard, the head of the government department Juk worked in. His boss's boss. *Or was there another layer?* Didn't matter, he'd make sure Juk learned how things worked.

"Hello?" Orson's deep voice came through the phone.

"Orson? It's Betsy."

"Betsy! My friend. It's been too long. Why don't you call me more often?" He sounded genuinely happy.

"Well, you always assign new pups to be my point-people. Why don't you give me someone I don't have to train?" She huffed in frustration.

"You're my best trainer, dear. Have been for years. A few years with you and I have the best international agents a department can ask for."

She grumbled. "That's not my job, Orson. And the last two you've given me are the worst. I called

Juk, told him I need to meet today. I said he could have one or two hours. He said to call through proper channels next time, and we could meet next week Thursday."

Orson scoffed. "Does the boy know it's Monday and that's a week and a half away?"

"I don't know."

"How important is this?"

Betsy rubbed her forehead. "In a level of one to five, it's about a twenty-seven."

He sighed. "Okay, meet in the main conference room in an hour and a half."

"Sounds perfect. Will you be there?"

"No, I'm in Maine. I can't get to the office in that time."

Betsy had explained her situation to him several times, but he didn't want to transport. "Okay, I'll let you know of the outcome, but I'm not holding my breath. This point-person isn't worthy of my time. You need to find someone better."

"Fine, fine. I'll put it on my to-do list."

Betsy and Viera walked into the government building just over an hour later. There was a desk blocking the stairs and elevator with two security officers. Betsy went to the first officer and gave their names, and they each showed their IDs. They were waved through to the elevator.

When they got to the correct floor, they headed to the room. They found only Juk waiting for them. Betsy clenched her jaw shut to avoid showing any other reaction at seeing only the young pup waiting for them.

He stood with a smile. "Ms. Doeth, lovely to see you. I wanted to apologize for any misunderstanding. I didn't understand when you stated you wanted to meet today that you meant today-today, and not, soon-today."

One of her brows rose. "For the record, when I say today, I *never* mean 'soon.' I mean *now.*"

They all sat, and Betsy wondered if getting a root canal would be less annoying and more productive.

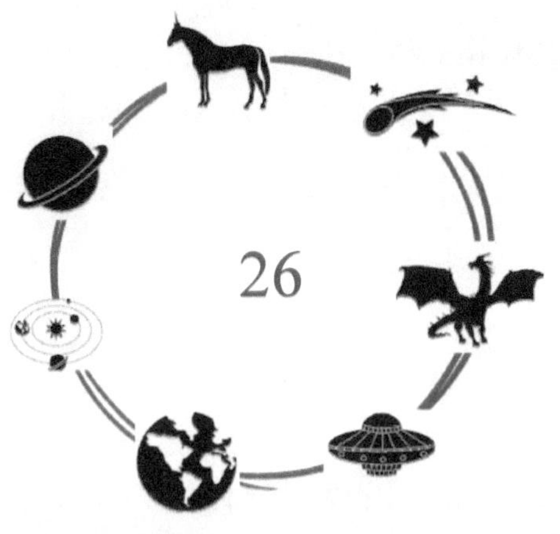

## 26

## School Yard Antics

### Viera

As the elevator zoomed up, Viera massaged her temples. Between depleting her magic and a heavy guilt at not being able to save Juniper, Viera felt dizzy and a bit nauseous. Both the space station and Abritos had different numbers of hours in a day, and she wasn't sure how many days her body thought she'd been away. She knew what the calendar said the date was and what the date had been when she'd left: two weeks. According to the people on Earth, she'd been gone for two weeks. With the weird different time frames, her body didn't know *what* it felt.

The elevators dumped them out into a waiting room with a stern looking woman in her thirties sitting behind a raised desk. She sat in front of a wall with the words Department of Interstellar Coexistence and Knowledge Sharing. The last time Viera had come, she'd been so nervous, she hadn't really thought about this department or its name. More than that, they'd been sent to a spare conference room three floors down, apparently not important enough for the main room.

Betsy plastered on a smile and walked past the woman.

The guard stood, then her eyes widened as she recognized my friend. "Pillar Doeth. Welcome, I'll bring you your favorite tea." Her gaze swung to Viera. "Do you also like chamomile?"

Viera smirked, realizing not everyone was as vapid as the two she'd met last time. "That would be great."

Before they went any further, Viera reached out and touched Betsy's arm. "Department of Interstellar Coexistence and Knowledge Sharing?"

A laugh burst out of Betsy. "One of the better names I've come up with, don't you think?"

"DICKS? You named this department DICKS?"

"Well, I'm often working with them, why not name the place after them?"

They both laughed as they made their way to the conference room. Juk had a condescending smile on his face as they walked in. Viera wasn't sure what Betsy had said to the man to get this meeting to happen, but there they were in the government building in downtown New York with the man himself.

"So, Juk, you made it?" Betsy actually sounded calm. Viera wasn't sure how she did it. Though Viera could keep a poker face when teaching her second-graders and Juk didn't seem that much older, the images of Juniper's ship exploding kept playing in her mind, and it was hard to not be emotional.

They all sat and the woman who guarded the entrance brought their tea. Juk looked confused, but Betsy just smiled and thanked her.

Seeming to want to control the room, Juk's smile widened. "You mentioned this was important. What's happening in our wide world that you feel this meeting had to happen today?" His brow furrowed and he flipped through his notes. "Didn't Viera head back to that space station a couple of weeks ago? Does it have to do with that? A paper report or an email would've been fine, you know. You do understand email, right?"

Betsy leaned back, her eyes steely. "When Viera and I were here last, we warned you that there was a krottel ship near Earth's space—"

"And we've been monitoring ever since, Ms. Doeth. Our space is clear of alien ships, we'd know if there was anything we needed to know of. Just because most humans don't know about aliens doesn't mean that those of us who do are also blind."

If Viera couldn't feel the ire flowing from her friend, she'd think Betsy were still calm as a cucumber. *I have to remember to never play poker with her. Though, with my magic ... No, that would be cheating.*

She shook her head, realizing he'd been totally off topic. He was going on and on like an egotistical bird. Betsy wanted to explain about a danger, not discuss his standing as an Earthling who knew about aliens. If he didn't slow down and listen, he'd get people hurt, or worse.

"Juk," Betsy snapped out, getting his attention. "Please let me finish."

The man smirked with one brow up but tilted his head towards them. *He was so respectful the first day. What the hell happened?*

*'That's a good question, but you need to think a bit quieter, my friend. I need to focus right now. We'll talk about this skill of yours later.'* Betsy's voice left her head, and it took everything Viera had in her to not react.

"There are at least two alien ships in Earth's orbit," Betsy continued. "You know about the chanzii ship, though they may have a second one up there by now. They've called one in, and it may be here. I don't know how far away it was. They're going to start evacuating their people. It will be a multi-year process, so, no," she held up a hand in a stop sign, "that isn't why we're here, so don't assume that's why I demanded an immediate audience."

"Do you want me to spread that information up the ladder?" Juk asked, shockingly respectful.

"You can. I'll be writing a report about that soon. I'll attach it in an email. You do know about attachments, right?" One of her eyebrows rose in question. "I have a few other things to focus on first." She rubbed the back of her neck. "When the ship we flew back from the space station on returned to Earth's space, we found a krottel ship hiding behind the moon."

"Wait, what?" Juk leaned forward. "That close?"

"Yes, that close. The Ziner and its crew tried to contact them, and the krottel wouldn't respond, yet again. When they sent an envoy, the krottel shot the ship down."

Juk blanched. "Did the chanzii lose anyone?"

Viera leaned forward. "You understand we're talking about a spaceship and being shot down ... in space. The void of space. Right? That isn't something a being survives. You understand that the krottel approached this situation not for peace, but to destroy the ship and whomever was on it." Viera realized she was yelling by the end and took a deep breath to calm herself. She shouldn't allow her hurt and frustration at Juniper's death to take over her common sense.

Betsy put her hand on Viera's arm. "I'll take it from here, friend." She turned to Juk. "That isn't the point. The krottel didn't come here under peaceful intentions. This planet isn't near any of the other alien planets. It was a choice they made, and we need to be wary."

Juk looked up from taking notes and tapped his pencil on the table. "I'll get our people on finding the ship and we'll send a message."

The wave of frustration from her friend punched into Viera. She had to brace herself as Betsy spoke. "Did you hear anything I said? They aren't communicating. We've tried multiple times. The last olive branch sent out ended with them shooting down one of the Ziner's shuttles."

Juk gave Betsy a patronizing look. "Right, but the krottel were the ones who kicked the chanzii off of their planet. They probably thought the shuttle was out to attack. They were just defending themselves. I'm sure they'll talk with us. They're here to negotiate. That's what our department does—we're experts."

Viera could see Betsy's jaw clench for a few moments. Viera felt equally upset. She had to force the tendrils of her magic under control before office supplies started getting destroyed. Finally, Betsy took a long breath in, then let it out. "Juk, you understand that we are here as your expert advisors. We aren't here to tell you what to react to, but *how* to approach these situations. You should be listening to what we tell you. We have the experience and understanding." She paused, letting her words sink in ... or not, if the blank look Juk gave her was any indication. Viera had seen that look on many student faces.

Betsy continued. "We need to be extremely careful. The krottel have a history of moving in on planets to take them over. They've kicked the native species out more than once. There is no good reason for them to be here. You understand this, right?"

He gave a small smile. "I'm sure we can figure this out. You've done your part. Thank you for bringing this to me. If that's it, I'll take this upstairs and see you next time. You'll call my assistant, right?"

Betsy snorted. "No, I absolutely will not call your assistant. If I don't call Orson's assistant, why the hell would I call yours, pup?"

They walked out, leaving Juk with his jaw practically on the table.

His shock was like the dessert after a really bad meal. Thinking about Juniper, she slumped. A really, really bad meal.

In the elevator, Betsy texted the Ziner and Horax transported them back to Wisconsin. They landed in Thorn's backyard. As soon as their feet hit the grass, Betsy grasped Viera's shoulders. "Viera, do you know how you spoke in my mind?"

"Um ... yes?" Despite it being summer, there was a cool breeze and Viera wanted to get inside.

"On the ship you were projecting ... big time. I got some of it, but you've been working with Flower Prancer a lot." Viera couldn't hold back the eye roll the name of her trainer induced. Betsy smiled at her reaction. "I know, he's an ass. But the thing is, he saw your premonition. As you pushed all your magic into the vastness of space, he demanded Juniper be pulled from the shuttle."

Chills of fear and shock attacked Viera's body, followed by numb hope. "What are you saying Betsy? Tell me in short monosyllabic words."

"Juniper is fine. She wasn't on the ship when it exploded. Between the two of you, that damn yonat and your brilliance, you saved her."

Tears flowed down Viera's face. She'd been holding back her emotions, trying not to think about the tragedy, but she finally let herself go. Betsy wrapped her in a hug and let her cry.

Once Viera got herself back under control, they found Thorn and Scout in the kitchen. They sat for lunch. Thorn made pasta with a meat sauce, Earth style, with a side of garlic bread. Comfort food.

As they ate, a tension grew in the air. The food started to feel heavy within her, though she felt more grounded with each bite she took.

The panel made a sound and Thorn headed over to it. Viera was distracted for a moment, realizing her panel didn't make any noises. *I wonder if that's a setting? Could I monkey with mine to make different sounds?? I probably shouldn't be thinking about this right now.*

Thorn tapped on the panel and a view-screen popped up. One of Viera's eyebrows went up.

Another thing she needed to learn about! But then her heart went cold. Nine images flickered on a three-by-three grid. Bipedal beasts, obviously alien, appeared in different areas around the world. The images on the screen rotated to different locations, so though there were nine pictures, they saw more than that many locations. Krottel.

The same pull she'd felt on the island all those weeks ago caused Viera's gut to clench. "We need to get to Chicago, now. That's where it's all going to go down."

Betsy tilted her head. "Not New York? Isn't it always New York?"

"I think they're going for the biggest city near us. Though the government sent out their message from New York, we've done more transporting. They're not attacking here because our area doesn't have enough bang for their buck, and when I say bang," Viera gazed at each of them, "I'm pretty sure I mean *bang*."

# 27

## Clinging To The Past To Get To The Future

### Viera

They all stared at the flashing screens that showed the krottel landing in all the major cities on Earth. Some scenes were as bright as day like in the Midwest, while in others it was night, with stars twinkling in the sky. In some of the shots, small ships floated above the cities.

Thorn tapped on the panel. "Horax, we need a full complement of battle-ready enforcers."

His deep voice filled the kitchen. "Where should I deploy them, Commander Firoza?"

Everyone turned to Viera. Betsy's hand covered hers. "How sure are you that we should go to Chicago?"

Viera nodded. "Very. I can't explain it. I can sense the krottel like I'm somehow connected to the hive. Not fully connected, but if they're an ocean, I'm a boat floating on their currents." She rubbed her temples, not sure she was making sense. "They're furious. They feel betrayed and lied to. They want to punish? I think." She shook her head. "I'm not positive, but I know it's Chicago."

Thorn tapped the panel. "Millennium Park, Chicago. When the images of Chicago flashed, I saw the Bean in the background."

"Got it, Commander Firoza. I'll contact all the leaders. They have to have seen what's going on. It'll probably take a few minutes. Get yourself ready. I'll transport you in ten minutes. I'm transmitting your uniform to your room now."

"Send something for Betsy as well."

Viera bit her lip. "Me, too. I may not know much about fighting, but I want to be there."

Thorn's eyes narrowed as she seemed to look into Viera. She finally nodded. "Viera, too."

"Got it."

After he signed off, the three headed to Thorn's room and found the tactical outfits. They changed quickly.

Determination poured from Betsy. "Viera, I know you have a lot of power in you, but I want you to let others do the fighting. You're new to this world. The rest of us have done a lot more training. You're the backup, okay?"

The words felt like a punch in the gut, but she nodded. She knew her friend was right.

Once dressed, they only had a few minutes to wait until Horax, or someone on the ship, sent them to the park. As soon as they landed, Viera could feel the invaders. The city was filled with more than what the cameras were picking up.

All around her, Viera saw Thorn's people appearing and getting in line. Flower Prancer, Horax, and a couple of the other qynad from the ship also appeared. Viera knew this was the right spot, but a bud of fear blossomed in her gut. What if they all had come to the wrong city on her word?

Several of the krottel lifted shimmering black poles at least three feet long—or would the aliens measure it as a meters?—*focus Viera, that's not the point!* A beam came out of one of their weapons, flying towards a group of chanzii.

Viera thought her heart would stop, but the chanzii saw the attack and got out of the way. But the encounter was on. The qynad took to the air, fire erupting from their mouths, and the battle-trained chanzii fought back.

As the combatants spread out, Viera watched and backed up until she hit the Bean. She found Betsy in the crowd throwing some magic, and realized the other Pillars were near her doing their part. Several of the krottel exploded into their individual bugs, scurrying into the ground, some of them being destroyed in the process.

Bystanders not affiliated with the battle ran, screaming in fear. Viera laughed a bit hysterically as some of them squished the bugs under their feet in their haste to escape. Cars on the road screeched on their brakes to stop from hitting random people or other cars. Others held phones, obviously recording everything.

*Of course they are. If you don't get video, it didn't happen.* Her laughter got a bit higher in pitch.

The acrid smell of fire filled the air, and a shiver ran down Viera's back at the zapping sounds the silly laser sticks made.

Trembling, a feeling deep down shuddered within Viera each time a krottel was destroyed. Small pinpoints throughout her body. She saw a large red qynad flying above the city, shooting fire down to the street. As she watched, the fire disappeared behind the building. Pain traveled down her back. *The shot must have been successful.* She took a breath, trying to stay on her feet.

She scanned the sky but didn't see Horax's blue form anywhere above.

Viera closed her eyes, trying to block out the krottel. Deep down, she felt a glee coming from the bugs, despite the number of them not surviving the fight. *How many of Thorn's people aren't making it?* A lump developed in the back of Viera's throat. *I wish I could help, but I'm not built for battle.*

Digging deeper, she found an image ... the image that had brought them to Chicago. Viera opened her eyes. She'd seen a building with two noble lions standing sentry. She'd been on enough field trips with the school to know exactly which building that was. She ran.

Everyone seemed frozen as her super speed got her to the front of the Art Institute of Chicago in mere moments. But it was too late, the bomb was already sitting on the steps. "No! Stop!" She held up Gandalf's walking stick, which, as always appeared when she needed it, and threw up the biggest time bubble she could manage.

All around her, silence rang. The battle froze. She trembled as she rotated. Behind her a beam from a krottel weapon was inches from her back. Two other krottel and four chanzii fought in the street behind her, frozen where they stood. Weapons raised, ready to shoot.

There were humans holding their phones, recording everything.

*The Pillars' hope of keeping the aliens in the closet has obviously come to an end.*

With a sigh, she dropped her head back. Above her, the dragons had stopped moving as well. Viera shook with the power she'd expended. She turned and walked to the lion on the left. Next to it, on the steps, was a bomb engulfed in fire.

*What do I do now?*

She walked up to one of the chanzii. "What do you think? Should I carry you away like one of the superheroes in the movies?" She bent her knees and tugged. "Yeah, just what I thought. Stopping time doesn't suddenly give me super strength."

After a nervous chuckle, she held out the staff. "How about you, stick? Any ideas?" She waited a beat. "Didn't think so."

The magic drained from her, but she knew that bomb would take out half if not all of Chicago. This was too important. *Flower Prancer, why is this so hard? You need to teach me better!*

That's right! She'd call Flower Prancer. He'd know how to help. She walked back to the bomb. *'Flower Pracer, Flower Prancer, Flower Prancer!'* Each unanswered iteration of his name was louder than the last. Betsy had said she could talk to others this way, and he could hear her the best. *'God damn it, why haven't you ever taught me about telepathy? Damn it! Flower Prancer.'*

*'Quiet yourself, Ms. Kor, you are being impertinent. What is the matter? Telepathy is a skill which requires fine control, which you clearly do not possess.'*

Viera bit back a snarl. *'I'm looking at a bomb that's already gone off. Here is my location. Please hurry.'*

*'I may not have your speed—yet—but I do understand urgency, Ms. Kor.'*

It didn't take long for him to get to her. "I can't disintegrate it once it's gone off, it's too late. This is your city. What are you going to do?"

"Okay, I can do this." Viera closed her eyes and dug deep. With a bit of what they'd been practicing, she reversed the time for the bomb while trying to hold everything else in stasis. They both watched as the fire receded. As soon as the bomb casing was whole, the yonat did his magic ... literally. The bomb disintegrated, turning to gray dust.

"Viera, do you know which of the krottel are the leaders?" His violet eyes bored into her.

Her body trembled while she explained which bipedal creatures held the queens of the bugs. Their leaders.

Flower Prancer nodded. "Acceptable work, Ms. Kor. Once they're off the field of battle, you can release this time bubble."

Flower Prancer ran out of its sphere and contacted the Ziner. Viera assumed he told them the information she'd given him because five massive krottel disappeared from her awareness. She assumed they'd been transported away. With a sigh, she released her magic.

Feeling more like a rag doll than a person, she slumped on the steps of the Art Institute, half hidden from the combatants, and waited as the remaining krottel lost their ability to fight back. All around her, their bipedal constructs stood, motionless, waiting for their next command.

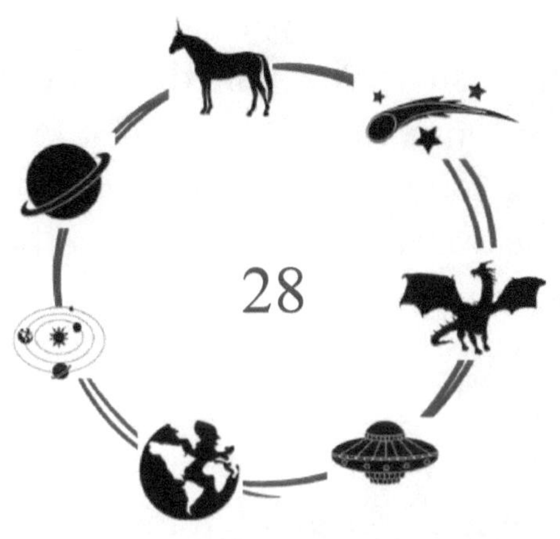

## 28

## A History Lesson

### Viera

The battle raged on while Viera sat on the steps of the Chicago Art Institute. She hid in the shadows, unable to help in any way. Since the krottel leaders had been captured, the fight probably didn't take as long as it felt, though she reasoned she could map it all out on her body as the bugs died and their final count could be notched on the pinpricks of pain along her arms and legs.

Eventually one of the chanzii she didn't know found her. "Ma'am, are you okay?"

"Yeah, mostly." She smiled weakly at her.

"You're Viera, right. The newest Pillar? You're living in the same area as Commander Firoza? Right?" The woman sounded concerned, though she kept looking around.

"Yeah. Why?"

She tapped something on her wrist. "I found her. The Elder was correct. She's okay but looks worn down. I suggest transporting her to Commander Firoza's house or the ship."

"Does she need help, or can she go alone?" Viera thought she recognized Juniper's voice and she immediately felt lighter.

Viera placed her hand on the other woman's arm. "I'll be fine on my own."

"I heard that," Juniper said, and Viera thought she could hear the other woman's smile. "Good to hear your voice, Pillar Kor. I'll get you to Commander Firoza's house." Before anything else was said, the world began to look like a watercolor painting. When it cleared up, she was on a couch in Thorn's living room.

Scout's voice came from the kitchen. "Ms. Kor? Is that you? Juniper said I should get you some hot chocolate. Is that true?"

Viera smiled. "That sounds perfect."

The next day, Betsy set up a meeting on the Ziner. Thorn's people didn't want to bring the krottel leaders back down to Earth. They felt bringing the human leaders up to the ship would be safer for the planet. Despite his reservations, Mr. Mard, leader of the Department of Interstellar Coexistence and Knowledge Sharing, was there, as was Juk, the dick.

Horax, Flower Prancer, Thorn, Betsy, Zuza, Ania, and Viera were all there as well. A few other international government officials were there, but Viera didn't catch their names. She felt like a small fish in an ocean of important people. She figured she was there because she was at the right place at the wrong time.

Flower Prancer stood at the head of the table. "We want to start this meeting by asking the krottel why they've been ignoring all forms of communication and decided to initiate contact in two instances with violence. First with the shuttle and then with Earth."

Juk's eyes narrowed. "Do you know the chaos you've unleashed on the entire planet? There is no turning back from what you've done." He turned his glare on Thorn and Horax. "Not to mention you two. You confirmed everything. We can't do any kind of cover up with what you did in Chicago, now can we?"

Viera's anger exploded like the bomb she'd stopped. "Do you even know all the details? Do you know about the bomb that would've taken out the city? Do you know that without the actions of this group, the one you've been disrespecting for weeks, millions of Americans would be dead right now?" Everyone gaped at her, and she sat back, trying to calm down.

"Yes, Ms. Kor is correct." Flower Prancer continued. "I was going to get to that." He searched the faces of the beings around the table. "I ask again. What were you trying to achieve?"

There were two of the krottel at the table. Viera knew there were more on the ship, but apparently, that was all that were invited to the table. The one on the left tilted its head. "You told us the Earthlings didn't know about aliens. We came to observe. We didn't feel we needed to discuss our plans with you, Elder."

Everyone waited, but apparently, that was all it was going to say.

With a swish of his tail, Flower Prancer continued. "Then why did you attack first this ship and then Earth?"

"You lied. The Earthlings knew where we were. They knew we were aliens, which means they know *about* aliens. If they know about aliens, then their world is fair game." It rotated to stare more directly at Juk. "It was you. You sent us a message. You said you were with the rulers of the land and wanted to talk. If the rulers know about us, then the people must know as well. That's how it works."

"No," Flower Prancer snarled. "That is *not* how this works. You are a hive mind where all your members know what the others know. Very few creatures work that way. For most of us, we need to communicate to know what is happening. On Earth, the existence of aliens isn't known ... or wasn't known, to the general public. Because you decided you knew best, you've changed it for their whole population."

"We need a planet. We need the magic. You lied to us."

Viera could feel the frustration from everyone in the room. Betsy scooted her chair back a bit. "You know that our planet is not an option. Why would you even come here?"

"We'll die out without the magic."

Thorn turned to them, her fury almost making it hard for Viera to breathe. "Where do you come from that you think you can just go planet to planet, kicking out the original inhabitants and then killing the world itself? Over and over?"

Viera could see the krottel tense. It could probably sense the emotions as well as she could. *I wonder if it can translate our feelings, so different from theirs.*

Its head swung around. "You want to know our history, chanzii?"

Thorn's jaw clenched. "Sure, why not."

It did a motion that could be called a shrug. "We come from the world Bhachana. Many years ago we lived happily, building our family, our colony. Life was peaceful away from the fire ... the sun."

Mr. Mard leaned forward. "You lived underground?"

"Yes, yes, underground, like the civilized." It made a chirping sound. "The zukacic, the two-footed on the land, thrived for many years. Our people and theirs didn't interact while they lived. We found books that traced their history for centuries. We don't know what a cycle of Bhachana is compared to other worlds. Time has a different meaning to us." It paused as if they'd be shocked at this revelation. When nothing happened, it continued. "The ground above our head started to shake. It got worse. Then one day, we felt sluggish. We had my workers go and investigate. The land above was ... it was in ruins. No life remained."

Zuza rubbed his chin. "How old are you?"

"We told you," it snapped out. "Time doesn't mean much to us. We are as old as we need to be," it huffed. "We searched. There were no two-footers on the planet. When we found books, we learned how to read. When we found reels, we learned how to watch the screens. The two-footers fought. After years of peace, they fought ... no one survived."

Betsy, who somehow had a pad of paper, looked up from what she was writing. "How did you go from being bugs dying on a planet to attacking people on my planet?"

"We studied. The two-footers were studying intergalactic travel. We adapted and mastered what they'd started. We found this shape worked better for the ships. It takes what you call magic to maintain, but it's required for respect and using the technology. We felt weaker and weaker; we had to leave the planet. We would die." There was a pause. Then the krottel sighed. "We found another planet and at first we felt good. But then we all felt weak again. We had to try over again."

Before they could continue, before Betsy or Zuza could ask another question, before Viera could completely wrap her head around everything she'd heard, Flower Prancer swished his tail in annoyance. "You idiots. Did it never occur to you that maintaining that form would use more magic? Do you even know where magic comes from?"

The krottel's body tensed more, if that was possible. "From planets, of course."

"You're dumber than I thought. If it came from planets, you wouldn't have to leave that first one you left, now would you? Why am I always surrounded by morons?" He snuffled in frustration. "Magic comes from the living. Every time you ran off the living inhabitants of a planet, you destroyed not only the source of the magic, what you'd been seeking, you killed the planet itself. Earth is so rich in magic because there are so many people and so few magic users."

Everyone at the table sat stunned. Viera turned to Betsy. "Did you know any of that?"

She shrugged. "I hadn't thought about it."

The yonat continued. "You've been bungling across the galaxy instead of asking the Elders for help. You've been around for long enough to know how the different creatures work. Why wouldn't you just ask? You are such an arrogant ass of a creature."

Viera could feel the shock and frustration in the room shift to amusement at Flower Prancer's words.

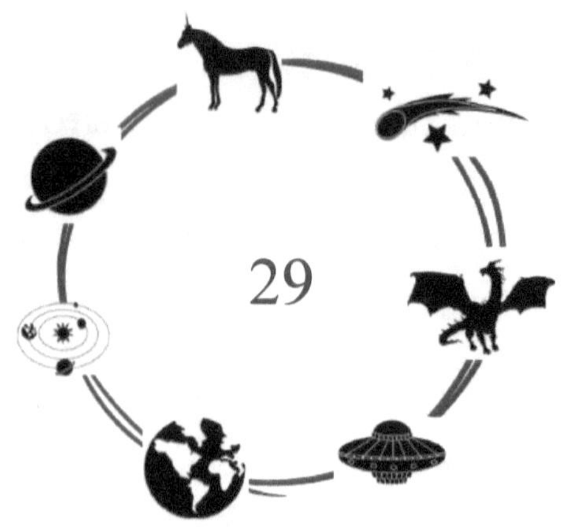

# 29

## Enemies to ... Maybe Not Enemies

### Thorn

The krottel sat there silent. Anger burned through Thorn. All these years her people had been displaced by these bugs, literally for no reason beyond their ignorance.

She decided to be angry at the obnoxious Elder. "Did you know that this was what was killing the planets? If they gave up this stupid bipedal form, could they live on a planet with the current inhabitants? Is this information you could've given earlier?" She forced herself not to yell.

As if moving in slow motion, the glowing violet eyes of the yonat turned to her. "The source of magic on planets isn't considered top secret, Commander Firoza. It never occurred to me that you or any of the others hadn't considered that in your dealings with the krottel. If you remember, it was only recently that we even learned the true form of the species."

His words hit her like ice water, and she immediately slumped in her seat. "You're correct, Elder, and I'm sorry for my outburst. This whole situation, both on my planet and Earth, has just put me in a very scattered position."

"I suggest regrouping, and fast, Commander Firoza. You are a leader, and as such, you don't have room for these kinds of mistakes."

Chastised, she just gave a single nod.

The krottel finally spoke up. "Where does that leave us?"

Mr. Mard tilted his head at the strange alien. "Do you like taking the bipedal form you're currently in?"

There was another pause as if the krottel had to communicate with its community before giving its consensus. "No, Earthling, we do not. We prefer our natural form. It has been a long time since we've felt safe that way. First we needed this form to master the two-footed reading and technology. Then, once we took over planets, we needed it to maintain dominance. In our ideal situation, we'd go back to the dark and build a community there."

Thorn leaned forward. "You seem awfully quick to agree to giving up your latest intergalactic pursuits. You're willing to throw in the towel, so to speak, and live the simple life?"

The krottel made a strange noise. "Why would we take time to decide to do what we've wanted all these years?"

Viera cleared her throat. "I can feel they want to be separate and away from space. They've had that goal for years. They are such simple beings."

Mr. Mard nodded slowly. "And are you like the Earthlings and chanzii where you want to all be together? Are you one colony?"

Again they waited. Thorn wasn't sure if it was a language barrier or a conceptual one. Maybe Viera with her odd connection to the krottel could get the concept across easier, but Thorn didn't want to strengthen that link.

Finally, the krottel's head bobbed. "We have five queens, as you'd call them. We all get along well and could cohabitate on the same world. We could also split up and live on different worlds. Our beings, as you call them, are long-lived. I remember Bhachana when the zukacic were still there. Not all of our beings do, but several are of an age with me."

Thorn wasn't sure of the timeline, but she thought that may be older than dirt.

Flower Prancer nodded. "I believe we could take one line of your krottel to our planet. I will speak with the dwarves. They are often willing to take on refugees. Like us, probably only one, maybe two of the smaller clans. That still leaves two or three of the groups."

Horax chuckled. "The qynad have lots of land. It's rocky and mountainous. I can speak with the governing body about sharing a bit with the krottel. We don't have a history with your antics, so that will help."

Thorn shivered, not understanding everyone's willingness to just let these bugs onto their planet. They'd done too much damage in her opinion.

"What do you do underground? Are you harmful to the planet?"

The krottel, who'd been silent, turned to Thorn. "No. We heal. We love the planet and try to make things grow. Destruction is anathema to who we are. The planets we've destroyed will forever be a dark spot in our history we will mourn."

Viera's head perked up. "Oh, that's sadness. I've been unsure how to translate your ... well, you."

"Yes, Earthling. You are confusing to us, as well."

Thorn worked to not react at the idea the bugs were reading Viera. It wasn't malicious. She nodded at the krottel leader. "Me or Flower Prancer can bring your request to Torville Station Number Six. I'm sure we can find other planets who will be willing to take you in, maybe even several in the same system. The number who took my people in during our time of need was overwhelmingly heartwarming. I'm sure planets can be found for you."

*Just stay far away from Abritos and Earth. I don't want to see you or hear about you ever again.*

"And," Mr. Mard added, "I'm assuming once you're all safely situated on your new planets, you won't be flying off anymore? Can we get it in writing that you'll be land-bound? Or planet-bound?"

The krottel took a moment before finally turning to him. "Are you saying you want us imprisoned wherever we end up?"

He shrugged. "You've killed and destroyed planets. You displaced the chanzii for years. And now, God above, do you have any idea what you've done to my planet? They didn't know about aliens or magic, and in a couple of hours you've caused havoc and mayhem on a global scale. We're all up here dealing with you, but in reality the work down there is just beginning. It's going to be a nightmare, all because of your arrogance and ignorance."

Thorn smiled. "Not to mention, you keep saying you don't want to be in space. Isn't having a permanent home your goal?"

The silence lasted longer. The queen spoke with her other bugs. Finally, it said, "As long as where we are is providing the magic we need to survive, we can agree to those conditions."

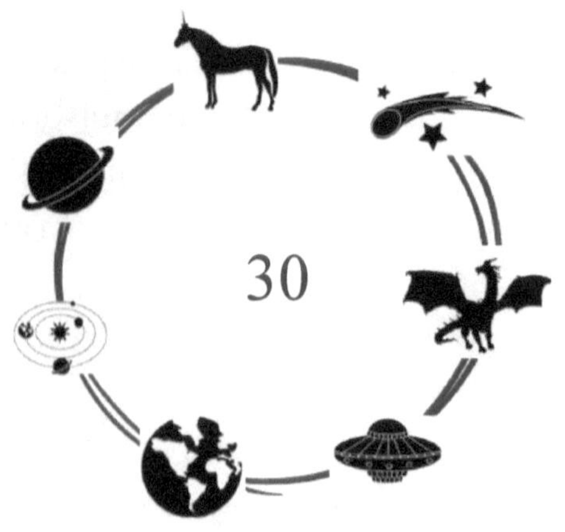

## 30

A Decision To Make

Viera

Viera sat in her kitchen drinking coffee and eating a plate of pancakes. She had a bunch of things to do today and hoped the first items would put everyone in a good mood.

Her phone rang. She checked the display and sighed. "Hi, Mother."

"Viera, are you okay? There was a bunch of stuff happening in Chicago. I know that's close to you."

She took a sip of her coffee and leaned back in her seat. "I'm fine, Mother. I'm a few hours north of Chicago. Everything's right as rain."

Her mom's voice got muffled. "I told you everything was fine." She obviously removed her hand from the receiver. "So, when do we meet this lady friend of yours? Your dad explained it all to me. We've even had dinner with your Aunt Dotty and her wife."

Viera was glad she was sitting and not holding her coffee. Getting burned wasn't on her long list of items for the day. "That's great, Mother. I, ah ... I'll see what I can do. I just, I just wanted to tell you ... I'm not sure what I wanted to tell you. Maybe I'll visit next week."

"Oh! So soon? Can you get a flight out here?" Mother sounded so hopeful.

She bit back a laugh thinking about how fast she could get there. She imagined popping into the living room and yelling 'boo!' and then disappearing. "Yeah, I think I can. I'll let you know after I speak with—" She heard her front door open. "Mother, I have to go. Betsy is here. We have a thing we have to do. I'll talk with you in a few days."

"Okay. Love you, dear."

Betsy walked in as she hung up. "Sounds like you had a heart-to-heart with your mom."

Viera's head dropped into her crossed arms on the table. She had things to tell everyone: her mother, Thorn, and Betsy. *I can do this! I faced a krottel bomb. After that, what can't I do?* "I don't know how I'm going to do this." She hadn't meant to say that out loud.

"Well, we'll start with going to the press conference. Maybe she'll be watching, and half your job will be done for you." That thought amused her. Though if it wasn't one of her daytime stories, her mother probably wasn't watching.

Lifting her head, Viera finished the last bite of pancake and washed it down with her coffee. "I should be so lucky." She placed the dishes in the sink. "So, is the press conference in Chicago or New York? I didn't get the details."

"New York. Orson wants to be there. He relented on transporting to the meeting with the krottel, but that was his limit."

Viera winked. "He survived the one round trip, and he's out. No more gambling?"

"Exactly."

After cleaning the mug and plate, Viera leaned against the counter. "I need to tell you something, and now is as good a time as any."

One of Betsy's brows shot up. "Oh, and what's that, my friend?"

"I'm ..." Viera paused, unsure of how to say this. She swallowed, trying to get moisture into her dry mouth. "Look, I know there are only five Pillars on Earth, but I love Thorn and they don't have any wizards on Abritos."

A smile grew on Betsy's face, bigger with every word Viera said. "You're going with the chanzii when they leave." It wasn't a question.

"Yeah. And since Thorn is in the first wave, I'll be leaving in the next month. I plan on volunteering to watch the kids while the adults focus on rebuilding their society."

Betsy wrapped her in a hug. "Oh, Viera! I think that's fantastic. I'm so happy for you."

There was a knock on the door before Thorn came in. "What's the party?"

Warmth and excitement bubbled in Viera as she gazed at the woman she loved. "Well, my beautiful friend ..."

Thorn's face scrunched up. "Friend?"

Viera waved her hands. "Let me finish or I'll never get this out."

Rolling her eyes, Thorn just nodded her assent. "Go ahead."

"Okay, here it goes." Viera's hands shook. "Before I follow the woman I love to a completely different planet," she watched as Thorn's eyes widened and her jaw dropped, "my parents would like to meet you."

Thorn lifted her in a hug, spinning them both. Betsy laughed; her joy filled the kitchen.

They didn't have long before the Ziner crew sent them to New York. They landed in the conference room where they'd had their meetings with Juk.

Mr. Mard walked in. "Alright, ladies. Are you ready? It's time to let the world know the truth."

As happy as he sounded, Viera was worried. The world was about to learn some very hard truths.

"Hi, my name is Betsy Doeth. I am what is known as a Pillar on Earth. Currently there are five

Pillars who have been keeping Earth safe for generations. I'll give you more information about what that means later. I am joined on stage by Viera Kor, Thorn Firoza, and Orson Mard." Betsy spoke to a huge crowd. There were thousands of people there to hear them speak. Speckled throughout the crowd were cameras.

"We are here to talk to you about what happened the other day all over the planet, but specifically in Chicago, since that is where three of the four of us were." She waved her hand at everyone but Mr. Mard.

"You mean when the aliens and dragons attacked?" someone in the crowd yelled.

Betsy laughed. "Yes, that's exactly what I'm talking about. Though, you do know you shouldn't believe everything you see on the internet." She waited for the laughter to die down. "On Monday, an alien race invaded Earth. Despite that, as a planet, we don't need to worry. There is a division of the government and specialists that have been working with another group of aliens for some time. Together, in a joint force, we came together to ensure the safety of our world."

Someone in the mass of people yelled, "What makes you so special?"

"I'm glad you asked." Betsy's smile remained on her face. Viera could tell she was enjoying herself, despite the centuries the Pillars had avoided just this. "Each of us have a reason we were part of the team on the ground in Chicago, the main area of the fight. Over the next few weeks and months we'll be holding more of these press conferences to give detailed information to all of you. In these sessions, we'll be introducing you to the individuals who were part of the team and maybe to some of the alien races who helped to keep Earth safe. Today, you'll meet the three of us. Mr. Mard is our government contact. He can speak if he wants at the end, but for now, I'd like Ms. Thorn Firoza to share her story."

Thorn stepped up. The crowd reacted as one would expect, applause, cat calls, and cheers. Thorn took it in stride. "Hello, people of Earth!" She waved. "I've always wanted to do that." Her smile grew, intensifying her beauty. "As my friend here said, my name is Thorn Firoza, or as my people say, Commander Firoza. I am from a different planet, a world called Abritos." In a quick transition, she dropped her human image. Her turquoise skin glowed in the morning sun, set off by her dark purple hair.

After a moment of stunned silence, the audience oohed and aahed. "I came to this planet when mine was invaded. Your government let a portion of my people settle here as refugees. Our planet has recently been emptied of its invaders and my people can return home. From the bottom of my heart, we chanzii want to thank you all."

The silence that followed her words was almost deafening. Then, slowly, people shut their mouths, which hung open in shock, and applauded.

Thorn handed Viera the microphone. "Hi, everyone. My name is Viera ... ah, Viera Kor. There isn't a lot special about me. I taught second grade for years." She shot Betsy a glance and her friend nodded emphatically. Viera wasn't sure why they'd decided she should do this, but it was time. "Betsy mentioned there were five Pillars here on Earth. They are wizards, or magic users. I would be the sixth, but I'm heading to Abritos to help them rebuild. I was included in the group of specialists because I am one of only six humans who can wield actual magic."

Viera held up her hands. She created the image of a dragon flying above the crowd. It morphed into a phoenix, then burst into a ball of fire. The heat could be felt by everyone below.

There was a moment of silence as everyone gaped at her and the magic she'd just wielded.

Someone in the middle of the mass of people laughed. "You think only six people on Earth can do magic? Arrogant much?"

A fireball flew from her hands, heat emanating from it. Viera was about to do something about it when it exploded into fireworks of pink flower petals that rained down over the crowd.

With a grimace, Viera shot a look at Betsy, lowering the microphone away from her mouth. "That was magic, I felt the power. You know I'm heading off-planet soon ... looks like you'll have a lot more on your plate than just aliens."

Thank you for reading!
Conflict Lessens

Please Leave a review for this book so others know how much you enjoyed reading it.

Find more information on my <u>books on my website</u>

About the Author

Harlowe Frost has been a teacher at both the high school and college level. Her parents instilled a love of reading from a young age. She grew up in the queer community. Her favorite genre growing up was fantasy and science fiction, that is, until she discovered urban fantasy and paranormal romance. What she never found in those books was the diversity in background, gender identity, and sexuality she saw in the people around her. She decided if she couldn't find that in what she read, then she would write it herself. This started her writing paranormal romance with a LGBTQ+ background.

Turn the page to enter the contemporary world of bakeries in Wisconsin.

A new book, coming soon.

# Bakery Wars
## By Hannah Willow

Chapter 1 - Hope Retreats

Val

The trees covering the hills up ahead looked so dark and foreboding. But, despite that, I couldn't keep the smile from my face and the excitement had me bouncing in my seat. I knew Craig would tell me to stop bouncing ... again. But I'd begged for this, and he'd finally said 'yes.'

"How much longer, do you think?"

I turned and smiled at the couple behind me. They both looked as happy as I was. I wish I could remember their names. They were a lesbian couple from ... Oshkosh? Oconomowoc? Oxford? One of those 'O' named cities. I was as bad at names as I was with locations. I really should be better; they'd been so nice to us since this began.

"Not long. If I remember from what I read, the time at the Center was two days to meditate, relax, and learn, and then we'd take a ride to the hot springs." My nose scrunched up as I tried to remember the brochure I'd read.

The man across the aisle—Greg? Tony? Fuck!—leaned over. "It should be about fifteen more minutes. Two days at the Center, a thirty-minute bus ride to the hot springs, and then we'll spend two days there in the cabins."

The pregnant woman, who sat behind me, sighed. "And do they expect all of us to have our babies in this two day window? There are seven of us on this retreat."

I laughed. "Can you imagine? Are you really due?"

She made a sound halfway between a laugh and a whimper. "God, I wish." Her hands began to massage her large belly, similar to mine. "I'm tired of being kicked. My due date is in three days, but my doctor said it wouldn't be for another week, maybe two." Her voice changed. "First births are notoriously late, don't expect your little one to show her face any time soon."

Groans from other pregnant women came from around us. From the back, one said, "Is that a script that they have to tell us all? Why give a forty week window if they really mean forty-one or forty-two? Gah! I just want this kid out of me."

That turned everyone's dour sounds to laughter.

From the front of the bus, the driver mumbled, "Whoa, what the—" Then his voice got louder. "Everyone, brace yourselves!"

The back of the bus slid to the right, towards the ditch, and Craig's arm wrapped around me. The bus didn't have seatbelts. Then I felt as well as saw the driver try to turn the steering wheel the other way. We crashed into something and I went weightless.

For a moment it felt ... glorious, then reality crashed back into me. Fuck! The bus ... an accident.

Then nothing made sense as people went flying around me. A foot to my temple, a seat corner to my back, and then I curled into a ball.

"I think this one's still alive."

Cool finger's touched my neck, my temple, my arm. "She is, but I don't know if we can keep her that way. I'm afraid, like the others, we need to save the baby."

"Babies," I croaked out.

"What?" The first person, a woman, leaned down.

"There are two ... twins." I tried to swallow. "Craig? Can I see Craig? Am I going to die? Will my babies die?" Tears streamed down my face.

"We will do everything we can to save your babies, ma'am," she said, and I saw the ceiling above me flash past: tile, tile, tile, light. Tile, tile, tile, light.

Rosy

A shiver ran down my spine as I gazed at the key in the center of the dining room table. *It's really real.* My hands trembled as I headed to the kitchen to make ramen noodles for dinner. I could afford to make something nicer ... like mac and cheese, but the belt would be tight until ... I gulped.

From the living room, Dad laughed. "Stop gaping at the key."

"But it's really real. Tomorrow we're opening up Roads Street Café and Bakery for the first time. It's ..."

"I know, sweetheart. It's been your dream."

I debated making coffee, but knew I needed to sleep. The grand opening of the bakery deserved me at my best.

A shiver of excitement wound its way down my spine at the thought *my bakery* and I managed to not giggle.

Just as I was about to turn off the light in the kitchen, my phone rang. Checking the display, I don't recognize the number. I debated ignoring it, but picked it up with a shrug. "Hello?"

"Ms. Roads?"

"Speaking." Years ago I read that you never said 'yes' in case phone trolls recorded the word and used it against you. I was always careful with my words.

"It's Divinity General Hospital. There has been a horrible accident." A boulder hit my stomach, and I sat. The administrator went on to explain about a pregnancy retreat with no adult survivors.

"We have ... well, several of the babies don't have any living family who we can find to take them in. You are on both the foster and  the adoption list. We'd like to place one of the babies with you, temporarily, to foster. If everything works out with you and the child, we will look into adoption."

My legs gave out and I sat hard on the seat. From the living room, Dad sounded worried when he said, "Rosy? Are you okay?"

Over the line, the man's words were insistent. "Ms. Roads, are you there? I'm afraid I need an answer."

"Yes."

## Chapter 2 - A Night On The Town

### Rosy

12 years later

"**M**om! Can I have the snickerdoodle pumpkin cookie? Oh, wait. I want the cookie that looks like a cup! I want the rainbow sugar cookie with strawberry sauce."

Smiling down at the small boy, the woman closed her eyes for a moment, then nodded. "Can you add to our order one each of what he asked for, and a red velvet stuffed cheesecake cookie for me? And a large coffee."

"Of course." Turning, I added the three individual cookies to her larger order. Her company had a standing order for the monthly meetings. I gave her a total and she handed me a credit card.

"The problem, Rosy, is you're too good at making cookies. Don't get me wrong, the rest of your offerings are amazing, but these cookies."

I laughed as she took her sweets and headed out of the store.

Before the door shut, Sacia blew in, her blond hair flying out behind her, blue eyes shining. "Mom, that's it! I'm done! It's summer!"

Behind her, smiles equally big, Charlie and Pris trotted in. The three of them had been inseparable since they were babies. "Hello, my troublesome three musketeers."

Unlike Sacia, Charlie and Pris were twins, Charlotte and Priscilla. Despite that, they didn't look much alike. Charlie was a few inches shorter with straight dark hair and green eyes. Pris had strawberry blond hair and brown eyes. All three girls were kids of a bus crash that had killed their parents, so they called themselves the triplets, since none of them looked alike.

The twins had been adopted by a neighbor. We'd realized it a couple months after the fact at a local park. After that, we decided we'd bring the girls up with full disclosure. They'd been thick as thieves ever since.

Charlie scooted up to the display. "Mom said you couldn't get Sacia into the camp, is that right?"

From the back, Dad grunted. "A few calls fixed that. You'll all be out of our hair in a week, thank all that is good in the world."

All three girls squealed and I heard Dad chuckle. He loved the three as if they were all his granddaughters, doting on them all the time.

Pris spun. "Okay, let's head to our house and start planning."

Before I could say another word, they were gone, along with all their twelve-year-old whirlwind energy.

A few more customers came through the bakery before I heard Cindy's gusty sigh as she pushed open the door. "I can't believe you're still here."

Dad's heavy steps came up from the back. "Yes you can."

A smile broke out over Cindy's face and she winked at him. "True." Then her eyes narrowed at me, the crystal blue pinning me down. "You promised me we'd have tonight to celebrate."

"But—"

"No," she snapped out. "It's your birthday. Mitch said he'd watch Sacia. Come on."

Dad squeezed my shoulders. "I did, sweetie. I can finish up here and close up. Sacia's with her friends, and we'll hang out tonight. Go, get dressed up. You remember how to do that, right?"

I gazed down at my apron, stained with vanilla and covered with flour. "Fine. I'll go. But not too late. The morning crowd are my best customers."

Dad gave me a shove. "I can open as well. I'm up at four anyway. Just take a few hours and try to remember how to be young. You do know you're more than a mom and businesswoman, right?"

Cindy laughed as I grumbled, but I hung up the apron and followed my friend out.

We sat at a bar, one of Pekara's nicer ones. "I can't believe you convinced me to come here." I sipped the gin and tonic, relaxing back in the seat. "You know it isn't like I'll find anyone here. Not only do I know just about everyone around ... every woman is straight or unavailable, not to mention, you are in a committed relationship. Really, what's the point? You mix better drinks, and it would've been cheaper at your place."

Cindy lightly punched my shoulder. "Would you relax and have some fun? You haven't had a night out in ages. It's like the moment you got the bakery and Sacia, you decided to give up on you. Yes, our town is small. Maybe I should've dragged you closer to Milwaukee, but it is what it is."

I took another sip, admitting the drink went down well. "Fine, I'll stop complaining. Tonight *has* been fun." Looking over the faces of the people in the room, I recognized customers that would come in early for coffee and a treat. Some went for cookies, others for cupcakes. The bakery didn't have a huge selection, but what we created was all excellent.

A jolt to my shoulder and Cindy's laugh brought me back to our conversation. Cindy pointed with her chin. "Do you know her?" At the bar sat a woman with short brown hair, almost shaved on the sides, but longer on top. The tips were highlighted. She wore a dark business suit. In the low lighting it was hard to tell if it was blue or gray.

"I haven't seen her at the bakery. She must be driving through. Got lost on her way to Milwaukee or Madison ... or maybe Chicago. She doesn't really feel like a Pekara kind of gal."

"Go talk to her," Cindy urged, pushing my shoulder.

"What? No. She doesn't seem like she wants to be disturbed."

Cindy rolled her eyes. "She's at a bar. Just ... go."

Grumbling, I clenched my jaw tight as I stood, smoothed out my dress, wishing my stomach were flatter, and headed to the empty seat next to Ms. Power Suit.

Behind the bar, Tony quirked a smile. "Another gin and tonic, Rosy?"

After I forced my jaw to relax, I smiled. "Yeah, Tony, that would be great."

"I'll put it on Cindy's tab. Your bestie should be good for it on your birthday."

I closed my eyes and breathed slowly. *Was everyone in this town out to get me?*

"It's your birthday?" The woman next to me asked, her voice low and sultry.

Releasing my breath, I opened my eyes, and smiled at her. She was beautiful. Her makeup perfectly accented her cheek bones and luscious lips, lifted on one side in amusement. And her light green eyes sparked.

Tony placed the drink in front of me and I took a sip, trying not to tremble. "Yeah, birthday." I shook my head. I wasn't a teen anymore, I could do this. "Yes, I'm thirty-seven today." With a smile I lifted my glass in cheer.

She tapped her glass with mine. "Well, happy birthday, Rosy." My eyes widened, then I remembered Tony saying my name. "I'm Nora."

We both sipped our drinks, and my birthday got a lot better.